MEREDITH RESCE

FOUR SHORT STORIES

Four Short Stories : Falling For Maddie Grace; and Where There's Smoke

PO Box 880 Unley SA 5061

National Library of Australia Cataloguing-in-Publication entry

Creator: Resce, Meredith, 1963- author.

Title: Four short stories : Falling for Maddie Grace; and Where there's smoke / Meredith Resce.

ISBN: 9780994578655 (paperback)

Subjects: Short stories, Australian.
Romance fiction, Australian.

Dewey Number: A823.3

This is a work of fiction. Names, characters and incidents are either the product of the author's imagination or are used fictiously, and any resemblance to actual events or persons, living or dead, is entirely coincidental.

Falling *for* Maddie Grace

Falling For Maddie Grace

Golden Grain Publishing

PO Box 880 Unley SA 5061

ISBN 978-0-9945786-4-8(E-Book)

Christian Fiction; Romance.

Cover Photographs:
Romantic Happy Young Couple Kissing On the Beach at
Sunset ©Epic Stock Media
Australian Rules Football ©simez78
Storm Splashing Surf ©Vibrant Image Studio
A Soft Cloud Background with a Pastel Color ©BKK1982

Glossary of Australian Terms

Dear reader,

Some of you will be familiar with Australia, Australian Rules Football, and Aussie slang. Others of you will not. Even though there are many cultural similarities between Australia and other English-speaking countries, there are some differences, and I would love to give you a taste of our culture. I have included a glossary of Australianisms to help you as you read. I hope you enjoy the story:

Australian temperature is measured in degrees Celsius. 35 degrees is hot and uncomfortable (95 degrees F) and 20 degrees is pleasant and mild (68 degrees F).

The number one spectator sport in Australia is Australian Rules Football.

Football guernsey: Some football codes call their football jumpers a jersey. Aussie Rules tends to call it a guernsey. Both are names of a cow...

To mark the ball: When the ball is kicked, a player who catches it without it hitting the ground, or without it being touched first by another player, is said to have marked it, and that player awarded a free kick.

A screamer or speccie (spectacular mark): In some marking contests, several players will leap for the ball. Some players time their jump, and use the back of another player to launch them even higher. When they catch (mark) the ball, they usually fall to the ground with a great thud. The crowd go nuts over these sorts of speccies. Search You Tube for Aussie Rules Screamers and Speccies to get an idea.

Mobile: Cell phone

Tray-top ute: Ute is short for utility vehicle. In America they are called a truck.

Icy-pole: An ice-block or ice sweet treat on a stick made from flavored and colored water. (not ice cream)

Lolly bag: A bag of candy

Smart alec: A wise guy; someone who is irritating because they pretend to know everything

Good value: A colloquialism to describe a person who is fun and helpful

Pointy end of the season: That part of a sport's season where the finalists will be decided

Local GP: The general practitioner or family doctor

Loo: Bathroom

Flyspray: Spray can of insect poison

Fellas: slang for fellows, used in the context of the boys at a footy club

Journos: slang for journalist/reporter

Physio: Physiotherapist. All professional sports clubs have their own medical professionals.

Medal Count Night: In Australian Rules Football there is always a gala presentation dinner at the end of the season that is a glamorous affair. Votes cast by umpires during the season determine which player will win the best and fairest player of the year. In Australia, this medal is called the *Brownlow Medal.*

Obs: Slang used by medical staff that refers to medical observations that are taken regularly, such as blood pressure, temperature and pulse rate.

Boot: The trunk of a car

200 meters: Nearly 219 yards

10 meters: A little over 10 yards

To glam up: Take a lot of trouble over appearance and dress for a formal occasion.

Stuffed it up: Made a mess of things.

Hi-Viz: Uniforms that are made of bright iridescent material especially to make them clearly seen are said to be high visibility or hi-viz.

Fashion mags: The glossy women's magazines that feature celebrities and gossip.

Working Bee: The name given to a volunteer community effort to get a big job done.

Serviettes: Napkins.

You will notice that Australians often shorten words like obs, hi-viz, journos, physio. These are just a few examples. When I think about it, we tend to not like extra syllables.

Chapter One

Falling For Maddie Grace

This shouldn't be difficult. There are only a handful of people in the studio. My usual audience is between forty to seventy thousand screaming fans – and they're usually screaming at me, not for me.

Maddie Grace swallowed her nerves. *Who knew being a field umpire for a football game would lead to this?*

"If you would just step this way, Ms. Grace."

Maddie followed the stage director or producer or whatever he was. She wasn't familiar with a television studio or the crew who worked there.

"Just relax. When Suzanna asks you a question, all you have to do is answer naturally."

"Do I need to look at the camera?" Maddie asked.

"No. Just respond to Suzanna. Our crew will do the rest."

Maddie stepped to the middle of the set, and took her seat.

"Suzanna, this is Maddie Grace, our next guest." The stage manager introduced her.

Suzanna looked up briefly and gave a painted-on smile. "Hello."

Maddie felt the host's insincerity, but guessed she probably had people thrust towards her all day, every day, so managed to forgive her indifference. Maddie took a quick sip from the water glass on the coffee table in front of her in an attempt to calm her nerves.

"Back in five, four…"

One of the crew—director, producer, stage manager, someone—finished the count using their fingers. The small audience clapped enthusiastically, music magically played, and Suzanna, sprang to life.

"Today we are joined by Australia's first female professional league football umpire, Maddie Grace. Maddie, welcome to the show."

"Thanks for having me."

"So tell me, Maddie, why Australian Rules Football?"

Maddie smiled. This was an easy question. "Australian Rules football is the number one football code in this country— apologies to all the rugby and soccer fans."

There was some light laughter from the audience, and Maddie felt herself begin to relax.

"Best not start a soccer riot in the studio," Suzanna said. "Can we assume we have some Aussie Rules fans in the audience?"

There were a few loud cheers.

"But Maddie," Suzanna turned her focus back to her guest. "This is a male sport. Rough and dangerous."

"I'm only the umpire. I don't get anywhere near the physical contact."

"But doesn't it scare you? I mean some of those players are nearly seven feet tall."

"They're harmless, if you keep out of their way."

Maddie liked the way the audience laughed at what she said.

"What happens when you make a call they don't like?"

"The sport at this level is strictly monitored by match review panels, and there are heavy penalties for players who get reported and are found guilty of misconduct."

"And you have the power to report a player."

Maddie nodded and raised her eyebrows. "That I do."

Once again, the audience clapped and cheered. *This is fun.*

"What about the fans? Surely you've had abuse from some enthusiastic supporters who didn't like a call."

"I don't hear abuse. My job is to watch the play, make fast decisions, and facilitate the game."

"I have to say, you're very brave, running around on a field with eighteen strong men—"

"Thirty-six," Maddie said. "There are eighteen per side."

"Braver than I thought." This time the audience laughed at Suzanne's joke. "As I asked before, why a man's game?"

"Traditionally Australian Rules football has been a man's game, but in recent decades there have been women's leagues formed and played at high levels."

"But you umpire the professional men's league in this country. Why?"

"My dad has been a senior professional coach for many years. Since my mother died when I was three, my dad wanted me with him, so I was always at games and training and club social gatherings. My whole life has been men's football."

"You're not the only female umpire, I understand?"

"No, there are a few of us, but I'm the only one who has progressed far enough through the ranks to field umpire at the most senior level."

"With the finals series coming up next week, I understand you're hoping to be awarded some games, perhaps even the Grand Final."

"I've been training as hard as the rest of them, and so far, our review board has not had cause to speak to me about any bad decisions. I feel as if I'm well set to be the first female field umpire to be awarded a game—I hope games—in a final series."

"Well, I'm not sure there would be many women in this country who'd want your job. But it is another step for equality, having a woman succeed in a traditionally male arena."

"It pays well, too." Maddie grinned.

"You wouldn't catch me running about with a lot of sweaty men for any amount of money."

This comment from Suzanna brought loud laughter from the small audience, and Suzanna took the opportunity. "I guess on the other hand…" She waggled her eyebrows. More laughter.

"I assure you, they're never still long enough for me to see anything other than the way they engage in play." Maddie was chagrined to feel herself blushing and hoped the flush didn't show on camera. She knew many women gushed over the muscular players in their tight-fitting, sleeveless guernseys, but she had been around these men since she was a little girl. She moved amongst them as an equal—a professional sports person. She certainly respected the players enough to not objectify them by ogling their fine-looking bodies. *Oh, dear, I just admitted they have fine-looking bodies. I must be as bad as Suzanna and this giggling audience.*

"What about your relationship with the players? Anyone special you've gotten close too?"

Maddie frowned. "Well for a start with, I'm an umpire, so my relationship with the players is purely professional. There would be a serious conflict of interest if any umpire developed a personal relationship with a player. This is a professional sport. This is our job."

"So you aren't close to any of the players, like as a friend?"

Maddie paused for a moment. She knew several of them, back from when her father was their coach. In her late teens, she'd been as much a part of that team as Dad had been, and she had been close to the players, in a brother sister way. She went to training with the team, and acted as one of the support staff. That was where she'd first learned to umpire.

"Well, I'm sure that pause must mean something," Suzanna said. "Perhaps we'd better not push too far for fear of exposing something we shouldn't."

Maddie felt the heat rise in her face again. "I assure you there is nobody and nothing to expose. I am a professional."

"So you say," Suzanna said. "But I assure you, a beautiful woman like yourself, always in the company of virile active men… Well, perhaps we'd better leave it for now."

Maddie was furious by the insinuation, but refused to react. She had practiced self-control many a time when she was coming on and off the field while being abused by unhappy fans. She was not going to show Suzanna that the innuendo had ruffled her feathers.

"Thank you for coming onto the show, Maddie, and we wish you all the best for the upcoming finals. We will certainly watch out for you."

"Thank you so much for having me."

As Maddie left the set she was annoyed. This interview was supposed to have been about a female succeeding in a male dominated arena, not speculating about inappropriate relationships.

Thank goodness it's over. She put her shoulders back, lifted her head and walked from the studio. She was *not* going to think about finely cut muscles. She had a game to prepare for.

***

Maddie had only a split second to react. An errant kick launched the ball high and now it was heading directly towards her, along with a number of players, all eyes on the ball. She didn't panic but she needed to get out of the way, while still keeping her eyes on the play. She needed to know if one of the players caught the ball. It was her job to award the mark.

This is what she trained for. She ran backwards away from where the players were converging. Then it all came unstuck. She collided with someone, trod on something and the painful twist of her ankle took her to the ground, right under where the ball was coming down. The impact knocked the whistle from her mouth. The players still hadn't seen her, their eyes skyward, watching the flight of the ball. They couldn't see her, neither could they hear her. There was a terrific clash of bodies—not unusual, but something she usually viewed from a different perspective, a much safer position than from right beneath. She saw who marked the ball, but couldn't whistle to award the free.

Then one player, who'd taken a heavy hit in the marking contest, came crashing down on top of her. She heard a whooshing sound come from her mouth as his heavy frame knocked the wind out of her, and then his head hit hers.

She lost consciousness.

Chapter Two

"Rev, you okay?" Zac Beecham heard the voices speaking to him as his foggy brain floated back into focus. He blinked rapidly a couple of times to try to clear his thoughts. As he moved, he realized he'd fallen on another player.

"Easy, Rev." The team physio placed a hand on Zac's shoulder. He must have got knocked out in the last contest—the team medical staff wouldn't be on the field and talking to him otherwise. He fumbled around, trying to find his balance and a place to put his hands so he could push himself up from on top of the other player. He managed to arch his back and push himself upward, and saw the iridescent yellow uniform beneath him.

No, no, no!

He'd crushed an umpire.

Hope he doesn't take it out on me later. Then he recognized the umpire. "Maddie?" She was out cold and had blood on her face. His blood. It was streaming from his head, off his chin and dripping on her face. He brought his thumb up to wipe the drops of blood from her cheeks. "Maddie, are you all right?"

"Leave her now, Rev." The team doctor had his upper arm, and was trying to lift him off Maddie.

"Is she okay?" Zac asked, as he allowed himself to be guided away. "She looks pretty bad."

"Let the other medics help her. Let's see how much damage you've done to yourself."

Zac allowed the team medical staff to do their thing while he sat on the grass, dazed. Only one thing seemed to be on his mind. Would Maddie be all right? He answered questions and moved limbs and allowed himself to be stood up, all the while watching the other team's medics put an emergency neck brace on Maddie, and go through the routine necessary to put her on a stretcher. He didn't know how long it took, but eventually his support staff helped him walk off the playing field.

"Is Maddie going to be all right?" he asked again as he reached the gate that led down the race into his team change rooms.

"She's in good hands, Rev. Let's just get you checked out properly."

Zac cast one last worried glance in the direction of the motorized cart now stretchering Maddie from the field. He looked up and saw the cameras pointed in his direction. The sideline commentator seemed to be speaking into his microphone, reporting his every move. He turned his head and allowed himself to be guided from the public eye.

***

"You won't be playing for the next six weeks, at least," the doctor said to Zac when she came back into the examination cubicle at the city hospital.

"No great loss. This was the last game before the finals, and we weren't in the top eight anyway."

"Yes, well, I'm not a fan of men running around and knocking each other about then expecting me to patch them up. I'll be glad to see the end of the football season."

Zac didn't make any reply to the brusque comment. He was a professional sportsman which meant there were people who loved him, people who feared him, and people who thought he was stupid for playing the game at all. In the end, he didn't do it for any of them. He played because Australian Rules Football had always been his passion, and he was good at it.

"I wouldn't advise training either." The doctor's voice broke into his thoughts. "According to your notes, this is your third concussion this year. You can't afford another knock to the head."

"What about my ribs?" Zac resisted the urge to wince as he thought about the strong pain in his side.

"Hairline fracture to two of them. Any physical contact could break them properly and become a serious problem. So no training for at least six weeks, okay?"

"So if the MRI is clear, I can go home?"

"I'd like to keep you under observation for another couple of hours, just to make sure."

Zac sighed. He would like to have known how the game finished up. They hadn't made the finals, so his team was trying to salvage their professional pride by winning the last game of the season. He couldn't even check his phone—that was in his locker back at the stadium, along with his clothes.

And he wanted to know how Maddie had fared. He looked at the heart monitor clipped to his finger, and wondered if it was necessary. He was still dressed in his football shorts. His guernsey had been cut off to allow access to his ribs which were now carefully bound. The nurse had offered him a hospital gown, but he'd declined. The sheet would do for the time being. Max would get here soon with his gear. He'd better.

As if thinking about him had conjured him up, Zac's agent appeared at the door of the cubicle bearing Zac's sports bag.

"Good job we're not in the finals," Max said as he came into the room. "The fans would go nuts if you were sidelined at the pointy end of the season."

"Your concern for my wellbeing is overwhelming. Thank you."

"I take it you're okay," Max said. "The hospital staff didn't seem too worried."

"Cracked ribs, concussion."

"The usual, then?"

"Concussion is serious. Or so they have attempted to impress on me."

"Like I said, it's a good thing we're not in the finals. Your good looks are still intact, so at least we can see what advertising endorsements we can get for you."

"Do you know what happened to Maddie?" Zac asked.

"What's with that, Rev?" Max asked. "How come you're on first-name basis with one of the umpires? And the only female ref at that? The media are going crazy over it."

"I hope you told them to back off," Zac said, "and I wish you'd call me Zac. That is my name."

"I'm your manager, and Rev is what the fans call you. That is the name we trade by."

"Yeah, but it was meant as a derogatory name."

"Don't let the media get under your skin. It describes perfectly who you are. If I were you, I'd embrace it and make use of it."

"You know the media only used it because calling me a Bible-thumping religious fanatic took up too many characters in a headline."

"Zac, you are studying part time at a Bible college. Far from being the partying bad-boy of the football world, you're the complete opposite. I think the Reverend works well all the way round."

"A lot of professional sportsmen study part time, getting ready for a career after footy."

"How many of them are studying for a Bachelor of Christian Ministry degree?"

"Does it matter what I study?"

"Let it go, Zac. Your fans love you, they've adopted the name Rev, all the commentators use it. Embrace it and get as much from it as you can."

Easy for Max to say. The name still annoyed Zac. He wasn't ashamed of his ambition to work in Christian youth ministry one day, but he feared the fickle media were toying with him, that they took his other passion as nothing more than an opportunity to make fun of him.

"Anyway, you avoided the question," Max said. "What's with you and the umpire?"

"Nothing." Zac's voice sounded defensive, even in his own ears.

"All that tender emotion on the field, with the entire football world zoomed in. Calling her by her first name. Didn't look like nothing."

"I've known her for years," Zac said. "Her dad was my former coach."

"She's Jimmy Grace's daughter?"

Zac nodded. "She was a part of the support staff, and she learned to umpire during our training matches."

"Thank heavens," Max said. "I tell you, the images that went up on the big screen at the ground looked like she was your one true love."

Zac gave a well-performed laugh. But it wasn't funny. Maddie was one of the boys—sort of. He'd known her since she was in her teens, and knew her story. She'd had a nanny when she was younger, but by the time he knew her, she was her dad's shadow, mad about Australian Rules Football and part of the team. She would have played if she'd been allowed, but her father didn't coach a women's team, so she took up umpiring. Zac hadn't been following her career, but he was pleased she had succeeded to the highest level.

Except for today.

"You'd let me know if there was something more to this," Max said. "I can run interference with the media and put a good spin on it. You don't want to let them loose with a love story."

"There's nothing in it," Zac said again. "Besides, all the other blokes have girlfriends, and no one cares about their love lives until the red carpet at medal count night."

"They care about your private life, because you have this super good-boy image, and they're waiting for you to slip up."

"That's ridiculous."

"I'm just telling you. Let me know if there are any developments, so I can put a good spin on it before their collective imagination gets carried away."

"When I find a girlfriend, you'll be on my list of people to notify."

Chapter Three

By the time Maddie's foggy brain cleared, she was lying flat on her back in an MRI scanner. She had regained consciousness while she was being loaded into the back of the ambulance, but she hadn't been able to think clearly. Now she had to lie perfectly still and had plenty of time to review the incident in her mind. She couldn't remember how she'd fallen, nor how she was knocked out, but she knew she'd been umpiring a game. She felt a flush of chagrin. Umpires didn't fall and get caught in play, and they didn't get carted from the ground on a stretcher-bearing motorized cart. She was familiar with the routine. In the past, she'd held up numerous games waiting for one player or another to be removed from the ground. This time, it was her. How embarrassing. And unprofessional.

As she emerged from the tests, scans and x-rays, she was met with her boss's administrative assistant.

"How're you holding up, Maddie?" he asked.

"Thumping headache."

"Is it serious?"

"Don't know yet. I'll have to wait for the results to come back. Listen, thanks for coming in."

"I needed to make sure all the Work Cover paperwork is sorted."

Maddie nodded.

"If you're okay now, I'll need to get back to the stadium. I've a heap of work I have to sort today. I'll get Ted to follow up after the game."

"Thanks again." Maddie watched as he walked out of the emergency department. It wasn't until the sliding automatic doors had closed behind him that she wished she'd asked him to get her sports bag sent from the stadium to the hospital. *Too late now.* She couldn't even call him, as her phone was in that bag. Her head felt like it might split in two, so Maddie relaxed back into the pillow on the hospital gurney, and closed her eyes.

"How are you feeling now?" Maddie jolted awake at the doctor's words. She was right next to the bed in the treatment cubicle and took up the clipboard with her notes on it.

"Thumping headache, and something's not right with my left ankle."

"Yes, it looks like a bad sprain. Good news is you don't have any internal bleeding, but it is a concussion."

Maddie nodded.

"You're an umpire, I understand."

"Yes. It's my job."

"You won't be back on the field for at least a couple of weeks, depending on how the ankle heals."

Maddie didn't say anything. Now she had no chance of umpiring the final series.

"So you and Rev had a fair collision," the doctor said as she scribbled some notes. "Do you remember any of it?"

"Rev?"

"Zac Beecham. He asked after you."

"Is he okay?" Maddie asked. "He's a friend of my dad's."

"He came off better than you."

"So he's here, in this hospital?"

The doctor nodded. Maddie didn't push. She guessed it wasn't proper protocol to discuss another patient.

"Could I make a phone call?" Maddie asked. "I don't have my mobile with me."

"I'll get one of the nurses to organize something for you." The doctor hung her file on the end of the bed and left the cubicle.

***

"Hey, Max, can you come and pick me up when you get this message?"

Zac ended the call, frustrated that he'd not been able to contact Max after five calls.

He picked up the sports bag Max had brought in earlier. He'd have to take a taxi home. He went to the nurse's station.

"Is there anything I need to sign before leaving?" he asked. A young nurse looked up at him and blushed.

"You're the Rev?" she asked, obviously flustered at encountering a sports star. It happened sometimes, and Zac was used to being recognized. He nodded and waited for an answer, although she seemed to have forgotten the question. She gave her head a shake as if she'd just realized he was waiting.

"Oh, sorry. I'll just check." She broke her fan-gaze and went to find someone who did know the answer. Zac drummed his fingers on the counter and looked at the patient board. His name was still there, and down the list he saw Maddie Grace written in black marker-pen. He noted the bed number and waited for the nurse to come back.

"Is it okay if I visit Maddie Grace in bed twenty-five?"

The nurse looked disappointed, in a groupie kind of way.

15

"She's my former coach's daughter." Zac didn't know why he felt compelled to explain himself.

"If you just sign this paper, then you can visit who you like," she said.

"She's okay, then?"

"This is only emergency department, not intensive care."

Zac signed the paper. "Which way is bed twenty-five?"

"Down the corridor on the left." She pointed in the direction he should go.

Zac picked up his bag and hooked it on his shoulder with care, favoring his injured ribs. As he approached the door he heard Maddie's voice.

"I'll be all right, Dad," she said. "They want to keep me a couple more hours for observation, but I should be okay to go after."

There was a pause, and Zac tapped on her door and went in. She looked up at him and gave a small wave but maintained a serious expression.

"Dad, I have to go. Zac Beecham has just dropped in to visit." Pause. "How do you know he knocked me out?" Pause. "Dad, seriously? Okay, hold on." She held the portable phone handset toward Zac. "He wants to talk to you."

"Hi, Jimmy," Zac said. "I'm really sorry about what happened to Maddie."

"I saw it several times on replay," Jimmy replied. "They made quite a thing of it."

"Of what?" Zac asked.

"'Does the Rev have a girlfriend?' was the question asked on the postgame commentaries."

Zac didn't know what to say.

"Well, does he?" Jimmy asked.

"No!" Zac said. He was on the defense again.

"Good. So there's nothing going on?"

"No. I haven't seen Maddie in a couple of years. I didn't see her today either, or I wouldn't have run right over her and knocked her out."

"Yes, well. Since you're there, can you do me a favor?"

"Sure." Zac respected his former coach, and was responsible for Maddie's predicament.

"Our boys won today. We've made the finals which means I can't really fly down to Melbourne with this week being vital in finals preparation. But I don't want Maddie to be alone."

"Don't you have any family in Melbourne?" Zac asked.

"All our family is in Perth, and I'm in Brisbane. Maddie's grandparents aren't well enough to fly all the way over from Perth. She said she isn't too bad, and they'll send her home shortly. Could you make sure she gets back to the apartment, and stay with her tonight? Concussion, and all that."

Zac looked at his watch. It was already ten o'clock and Max still hadn't returned his call. There was a comfy recliner chair in the corner of the room. Sure, he could do Jimmy this favor and wait for Maddie.

"Okay," he said. "Do you think she'll mind?"

"Probably, but she needs someone with her. I'd prefer if I could talk to her doctor and make sure she really is okay. Could you do it?"

"I'm not family!" Maddie was watching him and frowning. She probably guessed what her father was saying. He was a strong take-charge personality—the sort who could take a professional football team to the finals.

"Make something up," Jimmy said. "Just make sure she isn't making light of the situation. I saw the blow several times in slow-motion. Even though the cameras were more interested in you, I saw how she looked when you were sitting on top of her, wiping blood from her face."

Zac felt the blood rise in his face. The details of the accident were still a little fuzzy in his mind. This was an on-field incident in an all-male sport, and yet somehow, Maddie had appeared, and now everybody seemed to want to make something of it.

"Maddie has my number. Call me once you've spoken to the doctor, okay?" It was Jimmy's usual no-nonsense tone. Zac knew that tone well. As a player in Jimmy's team, he'd never asked questions, but just done as he was told. He knew quick compliance would be the best policy now as well.

***

"He doesn't trust me, does he?" Maddie asked as Zac ended the phone call.

"He's just worried. Concussion is a serious business."

"You would know."

"He wants me to stay with you, and make sure you get home all right."

"I'll be okay, Zac. You don't need to stay." Maddie watched as several thoughts appeared to chase across his face. "Really. I'm sure the hospital staff will look after me."

"I promised your dad I'd talk to the doctor and see you home."

"What Dad doesn't know won't hurt him."

"Don't you want company?" Zac asked.

Maddie paused for a moment and took his full measure. She couldn't seem to read his motivation. "I just hate to keep you here for who knows how long. It's getting late, and you must have a headache as well."

Zac nodded. "I do, and my ribs are aching as well."

"Then go home and take some pain-killers."

"I feel bad about leaving you here alone, especially since I was the one who knocked you out."

"If it will make you feel any better, you can call me tomorrow to see how I am. If I need help, I'll tell you."

"Your dad seemed fairly sure that you wouldn't ask for help—a bit independent, I think he said."

Maddie laughed. Her father knew her well. She hated being mollycoddled.

"And besides," Zac said, "I don't have a ride home, so I might just as well relax in that recliner until the doctor comes, speak to him on your dad's behalf, and then we can catch a taxi home together."

Maddie shrugged. She had to admit it would be nice to have someone nearby who cared about her in a big-brother kind of way. Zac Beecham was like most of her dad's recruits. They all respected her and treated her as a legitimate sportsperson, though Zac had an edge on the others in that he was a Christian. Even if the others might have braved her father's wrath and tried something by way of a pass, Zac wouldn't. His media image was that of the good church boy. He was genuine. If he insisted on staying, she would enjoy knowing he was there for her.

"You'd better let the staff know you intend to stay," Maddie said. "They might come up with a coffee or something."

Zac nodded and left the room. Maddie was glad he'd insisted on staying. Having lived in Melbourne for less than a year, and most of that time taken up with either training or umpiring games, she didn't really have any friends to call in times of distress. Most of her colleagues were men. There were a few other girls who acted in various support positions in and around the football world, but they weren't the sort to go out for coffee or have a manicure together. Zac was actually the one person in Melbourne who knew her better than anyone else—like a sister. Her dad's players knew the boundaries, and they wouldn't dare step over them.

Zac walked back into her room.

"Well, that was incredibly awkward," he said, seating himself in the recliner.

"Don't they allow family to stay?" Maddie asked.

"Possibly, but I'm not family."

"You're the closest thing I've got to family here in Melbourne, as it happens," Maddie said. "But if they're going to give you a hard time over it, I'll be okay."

"It's fine. I can stay."

"Do you have medication for your pain?"

Zac nodded.

"Do you mind if I turn the light out and go to sleep?" Maddie asked.

"Maddie?" Something in Zac's tone made her worry.

"What?"

"They think that we're…you know…together."

"That's funny. Dad would kill you." Maddie gave a nervous laugh.

Zac didn't laugh.

"I'm only kidding. Dad wouldn't kill you."

"It's not that, it's just that…well, it's not just the hospital staff."

"What do you mean?"

"Max, my agent, tells me the media have gone silly about our supposed secret relationship."

"It's such a secret, neither of us know about it."

"You don't seem concerned." Zac's tone was somewhere between worried and relieved.

"It's only media speculation—gossip. Don't worry about it."

"You're right. They'll have forgotten about it by tomorrow."

"Have you got your mobile phone with you?" Maddie asked.

Zac nodded.

"Have you got a signal? Google the incident and let's see what the fuss is about."

Zac took a few minutes to let his search bring up a result.

"Anything there?" Maddie asked. She suddenly had that worried feeling again. His expression was tense as he stared at the screen. "What?"

"I don't think you want to see."

"Zac, you're scaring me. What is it?"

Zac seemed reluctant, but eventually let her have his phone. Maddie stared at it and frowned. There was a picture of Zac on top of her, touching her face, looking very tender and intense. She was speechless.

"I'm sorry," he said. "I was dazed, and there was blood on your face."

She looked up and saw the stitch on his eyebrow.

"It was an accident, Zac. I know it's not what it looks like."

"So you agree, it does look like…"

Maddie felt herself blush. She didn't want to discuss this out loud. Some clever photographer had used their telephoto equipment and captured a clear shot that made it look intimate, sensual. The blood rushed to Maddie's face again.

"Perhaps you'd better not stay after all," she said. "No telling what the media would make of that."

"It's too late," Zac said. He took his phone from her and scrolled through to another post. He gave it back to her for her to see.

REV SPENDS THE NIGHT

"This is just a report on your health update."

"Near the end of the report, they're saying that I could go home, but I've rushed to your bedside."

"Which is true—well not rushed, but you're here. I still think that by tomorrow morning, they will have moved on to something important."

"I'm really sorry."

"It's not your fault."

"So you don't feel upset by the speculation?"

"Well, it's all a bit embarrassing, but what I really feel upset about is that I tripped over during a match and got caught in play. I wanted to umpire the finals."

"I wanted to play in the finals."

"Well that's not gonna happen for either of us now."

>

It was nearly midnight when they were woken to be told the doctor had finally come to release Maddie. Zac didn't feel wonderful. His ribs hurt, his head hurt, his whole body hurt. He checked to see when he could take more painkillers.

"Zac, do you think you could go down to the stadium and get my sports bag from the change rooms?" Maddie asked. "I haven't got anything but this glamorous hospital gown to wear home."

"First, I'd better get a report from the doctor for your dad."

"Trust me, Zac. I'm old enough to deal with the doctor myself."

"Yeah, but I have to deal with your dad, and I don't think I'll ever be old enough to do that if I don't do what he's asked."

Maddie rolled her eyes.

The nursing staff had taken Maddie's obs, so all they needed was the doctor to clear her to go. He came in and took Zac's measure.

"You the partner?" he asked.

"For tonight," Zac replied.

The doctor shook his head. "Will you be taking Maddie home?"

Zac nodded.

"Good. Because she was out cold for a reasonable length of time, she'll need to have someone stay with her for at least another twenty-four hours," the doctor said. "Just watch for signs of concussion—excessive sleepiness, vomiting."

"I understand. I've dealt with concussion before."

"Given that her ankle is so swollen, it would be helpful to have someone to fetch and carry for her." The doctor finished writing notes then looked directly at Zac. "And nothing else. You'll have to wait for a few days for anything else."

Zac swallowed. He knew what the doctor meant. He should have said he wasn't Maddie's partner now, or ever, but he didn't want to have to explain why he was here listening to private information. He was too scared to look at Maddie, dreading her reaction to this. *Just get the information and get her out of here.*

"She'll need crutches with that ankle," the doctor said.

Maddie cleared her throat. "I am in the room. You can speak to me."

"I thought he was your partner."

"That doesn't mean I'm incapable of understanding what you're talking about."

"I've ordered a pair of crutches to be sent up for you. Once they're here, you can go." This time he addressed Maddie. "You can get changed back into your clothes while you wait."

The doctor signed a piece of paper and left the room.

"I'm sorry about that," Zac said. "I just thought it would be easier if I didn't make the relationship complicated."

"I get it," Maddie replied. "Zac, I have a problem. All my clothes are still in my locker back at the stadium. Is there any way night security would let you in to get my stuff?"

"Doubtful. Haven't you got anything to wear?"

"My sports shorts. They dispatched my shirt, for some reason."

"How come someone from the umpiring department didn't come with you?"

"Someone came with me when I was admitted, and filled in all the paperwork. I didn't think to ask him to get my bag, and I don't have my phone to call."

"I'm surprised your boss hasn't sent someone down to see how you're going."

Maddie shrugged. "I suppose he should have. I don't know why he hasn't."

"I've got a spare football jumper in my bag. You can wear that for the trip back to your place."

He unzipped his bag and pulled out his spare player guernsey. He always had a couple, just in case one got ripped during a game—which did happen sometimes, when a tackler only got hold of the jumper, and not the body.

Maddie edged her way off the bed, and went to stand up, but her foot was swollen and obviously painful.

"I need to go to the bathroom," she said.

"Let me give you a hand." Zac came close to her and let her take his arm. They shuffled across to the en-suite bathroom and Maddie let go, and took hold of the invalid rails.

"Can you get your spare shirt for me?" Maddie asked.

Zac stepped over to get it, and then handed it to her. She closed the door, and Zac felt a sudden wave of weakness. *What on earth am I doing? If anyone gets wind of this, it won't be any use trying to deny a relationship.*

The full impact of his actions hit him. Sure, he was following Jimmy's instructions, but no one here at the hospital would think they were anything other than a couple.

This is ridiculous. But then he began to think about Maddie as a woman, not one of the boys from the team. His mouth went dry again. *How did I get into this fix?* His thoughts were more of a desperate prayer. He probably should walk out of the hospital and leave Maddie to her own devices. She wasn't his responsibility. Her dad should have flown down to be with her. But…

But he wanted to be here, and he cared what happened. *What did that mean?*

***

As Zac walked out of the lift into the hospital main foyer, he saw no less than three reporters sitting about and drinking coffee. The slim hope their presence might be a coincidence at this time of the night vanished as they all turned his way and picked up cameras.

"Rev, did you stay the night with the umpire?"

"How long has the relationship been going on?"

"How does this fit with your hopes of becoming a priest?"

"I'm not going to become a priest!" Zac didn't have a chance to process each question before the next one was asked, but he managed to set that statement straight.

"So you've given up the idea of going into the seminary. Is it because of your relationship with Ms. Grace?"

"I was never going into the seminary," Zac replied. "I'm studying a bachelor of Christian Ministry, and hope to work as a Christian Youth worker following my football career."

"So how does your relationship with Ms. Grace affect that goal?"

"I don't have a relationship with Ms. Grace." Zac was getting frustrated.

"So you didn't spend the night with her?"

Zac hesitated. He didn't lie, but telling the truth would be like throwing fuel on a fire.

"Then you did spend the night with her?"

"Well, being as it's one in the morning, it's still technically night, and I'm going home. Anyway, I'm a friend of the family. Her father, as you know, coaches up in Brisbane. Jimmy was unable to come down to be with her, and asked me if I would stay with her during this difficult time."

"And how is Ms. Grace now, following your clash yesterday?"

"A little worse for wear, I'd say. Thank you for your interest. I have things I need to tend to."

Zac walked away in search of a taxi, pretending he couldn't hear the additional questions thrown his way. *Honestly, sometimes the hunt for a story can get right out of control.*

***

Zac's football guernsey was long enough on Maddie to make a neat mini-skirt. She couldn't even see her shorts underneath. She felt exposed, and as a nurse wheeled her through the hospital sliding doors, the early spring night air was cold, and gave her goose-bumps over her entire body.

"You must be freezing," Zac said as he approached and helped her out of the wheelchair.

Maddie nodded as she pulled the new crutches up under her arms, trying her best to balance.

"Here." Zac pulled his sports hoodie over his head and handed it to her. She saw his grimace. The simple action must have hurt his injured ribs. He helped to pull the hoodie over her head, and held her upright while she let go of one crutch and then the other to put her arms into the sleeves. The hoodie was as long as his guernsey, so her legs were still exposed to the cold night air. But she absorbed the warmth of his body that still clung to the jumper.

Maddie felt a strange sensation, a rush. She hoped it wasn't some nasty side effect of the concussion, but feared it might not have anything to do with her physical condition at all. It felt something akin to

26

warm and fuzzy and emotional. *What is that?* Zac was just doing what her father asked him to do, but it felt very much like he cared, in more than a brotherly way. She decided to keep the information to herself. It might not be a good development—neither of them could afford to be distracted by emotional entanglements.

He was incredibly attentive while Maddie shuffled and manoeuvred her way into the back seat of the waiting taxi. He handed her crutches in, then put his own sports bag in the boot of the taxi, and got into the front.

Maddie leaned forward to give the driver her address, and then they all fell silent for the ten minute drive. Being a city apartment, she didn't live far from either the sports stadium or the hospital.

They drew up to her apartment block, and she was glad to see the security guard as she didn't have her keys or purse or anything. Zac paid the taxi fare, and the security guard let them into her apartment.

"I'm really sorry that you have to do this," Maddie said to Zac, once they were inside and the door closed.

"I'm really sorry I knocked you out."

Maddie gave a weak smile.

"I remember who marked the ball. I was going to award the free."

"It wasn't me, was it?"

"No, you were way off. The television commentary would have loved that mark, though. It was a screamer, and spectacular."

"Except for those of us who ended up smashed in the contest, and out cold on the ground."

"The viewing public would have been all over it. It'll be registered for mark of the year."

Zac went quiet for a moment.

"You can sleep in Dad's room," Maddie said. "Do you need anything?"

"Maddie?"

"Yes."

"You know the media won't let this alone, don't you? It won't just be the marking contest that they'll replay to death."

"For a couple of days. The fans aren't interested in me. They're interested in you and your sporting ability."

"I hope you're right, but I've seen media storms erupt before, and this has the hallmarks of one brewing."

"Go to sleep, Zac. It will be okay in a couple of days."

"I'll set the alarm on my phone for every two hours. The doctor wants to make sure you don't go comatose."

"I'll set mine as well, in case your concussion is worse than they thought."

Zac smiled. "Do you need any help getting into bed?" he asked.

"I'll manage." *Seriously Zac, I'll manage. You're worried about a media storm. I'm more worried about an emotional storm. Let it go.*

Chapter Four

Zac woke to the sound of his phone ringing. He groaned, a mixture of pain and foggy brain and wishing he didn't have to wake up yet again. But this time it was the phone, not the alarm.

"Zac Beecham," he said, not trying to hide the sleepiness in his tone.

"Hi, this is Ted Hills. I'm wondering if you have Maddie Grace with you."

Ted Hills. The head of umpiring for the senior football league.

"Ah, yeah, Ted. She's still asleep."

"Would you mind waking her?"

"We've had a fairly rough night."

"I imagine. Still, I need to speak with her."

"Just a minute."

Zac was slow. The pain in his ribs was throbbing, and his head still ached. He dragged himself out of Jimmy's queen-sized bed, shuffled to the adjoining bedroom and knocked lightly on the door. There was no answer, so he opened it carefully, a little worried at the lack of reply.

"Maddie? You okay?"

He was relieved to see Maddie roll over and wake up.

"Ted Hills is on the phone." He walked across the room and held out his mobile phone for Maddie to take. He felt as if it wasn't his business to listen, so he walked out of the room and left her to it.

***

"Maddie, what's going on?"

Maddie struggled to get perspective. Her head was full of cotton wool, her body and foot ached, and she was still trying to figure out who was on the phone.

"You're sleeping with one of the players, Maddie. Do you know how serious this is?"

"What?" Adrenaline shot through her blood. Her mind was clear now.

"It's all over the papers. It breeches all professional ethics, calls into question our whole integrity as a governing body."

"Ted, stop!" Maddie pulled herself into a sitting position.

"If you'd started something, you should have let us know."

"I haven't started anything!" Maddie almost shouted, but then regretted the pain that coursed in her head. "I had an accident, and the people who should have been most concerned about me didn't even appear at the hospital."

"I called the hospital several times," Ted replied. "They told me you'd probably be kept in overnight, so I called again this morning to see if you needed someone to pick you up, and they told me that you'd gone home with your partner."

"He's not my partner." Maddie was flustered. "We're just friends."

"As a professional, you do know that we should have known that you had a relationship with one of the players. This is a serious conflict of interest."

"When I say friends, he played for my dad. I haven't caught up with him since he left Dad's team."

"That was not how it looked on the field yesterday. And he was with you in the hospital, and now you're in bed together."

"I'm in my bed, and Zac is in Dad's bed. There is nothing in this, Ted."

"I'm not convinced. When you wouldn't answer your phone, someone suggested I try Rev, and he hands the phone to you in your bed."

"My phone is still in my sports bag, in my locker down at the stadium. You might have thought to bring it to the hospital for me. Then you would have seen for yourself how I was and what I needed, and Zac wouldn't have needed to get involved."

Ted was quiet on the other end of the phone.

"Ted?"

"You won't be eligible to umpire the finals, Maddie. Not after yesterday."

The weight of disappointment sank like a cold stone inside Maddie's stomach. Her season was over. And maybe her career.

"I sprained my ankle in any case," she said.

"You got caught in a major on-field incident. I was considering you, but you know the nay-sayers have always said there's no room for women in men's football."

"I'm not the only umpire whose ever got caught in an on-field incident." Maddie suddenly felt the need to defend herself.

"You're the only umpire who's been involved in an intimate love exchange in front of a stadium full of fans."

"It wasn't what it looked like."

"Nonetheless, the leadership group feel it's best to drop you from the seniors."

"He knocked me out. I didn't have anything to do with it."

"This time he knocked you out, next time, he might knock you up."

Maddie couldn't find any words. She knew that men used coarse language all the time, and she'd hardened herself to it. If she wanted to work in a man's world, she had to toughen up—but the insinuation was a character judgement on both her and Zac. This didn't affect just her. Zac's good name was on the line here as well.

"Maddie?"

"That statement was unnecessary and offensive," Maddie said. "You should apologize."

"I can apologize, Maddie, but it is the joke that's being bandied around. You need to understand how this thing is being perceived."

"It's not my style, Ted, but you need to warn the others that sort of talk is a sexual harassment case waiting to happen. And you should consider that demoting me on the strength of gutter talk is sex discrimination."

"Noted."

Maddie sighed.

"Obviously I won't be back on field again this season, but please put a lid on all this talk about Zac and me. It's stupid and destructive to both our careers."

"If I were you, I'd get him out of your apartment as soon as you can."

"Believe me, it is the first thing on my agenda."

***

Zac was awake. He could hear Maddie was upset by the tone that filtered through, and he guessed what Ted was saying. He heard her trying to get her crutches ready to walk, so knocked on her door again.

"Are you okay?" he asked, peering into the room.

Maddie looked up, and opened her mouth as if to speak, but the words wouldn't come. She looked helplessly at him, shook her head, and then, to his horror, she began to tear up. This was way out of his league. He'd never had trouble relating to Maddie before, as a sportsperson, as one of the boys, but tears… this was foreign ground. To make matters worse, Maddie was dressed in short pyjamas that highlighted every one of her remarkable feminine features. This was no sportsman standing before him.

"What did he say?" Zac asked, swallowing hard.

"He's threatening to drop me from the senior league."

"Because of the accident?"

"Because of you…you and me…together…but we're not…but they don't care…just how it looks…and they're joking about it."

"Joking? What do you mean?"

Maddie ducked her head, as if trying to hide her emotions.

"It doesn't matter, Maddie," Zac said. "They'll forget it in a week or so."

Maddie plopped back onto the bed, and her face crumpled. Zac felt awful. He didn't know whether to go to her or leave her alone. He elected to sit down next to her, and put his hand on her shoulder, but that was met with a dramatic response.

"No, Zac. That makes it worse."

"I'm sorry," he said. "I'm not trying to make it worse. You just look really upset."

"I am upset. You should have heard what they're saying."

"What are they saying?"

Maddie didn't answer, so Zac got up, picked up his mobile phone and began to do a search on his name. He found it.

THE REV'S FALL ON GRACE
THE REV SLEEPS WITH THE REF
THE REV'S SECRET LOVE EXPOSED

The headlines rolled on. He had known there was a media storm in this. He checked his social media and found all manner of responses. He might have laughed at half of them if Maddie hadn't looked so miserable. Some female fans were lamenting he was no longer available, others thought Maddie was a conniving cow who didn't deserve him, while footy fans ranted about corruption in the umpiring world, and feminists screamed foul that Maddie was being sexualized and persecuted just because she was a woman.

"It's not funny, Zac." Zac looked up. He hadn't realized that he must have smiled at some of the more ridiculous comments.

"I know. I'm sorry, but some of the stuff that people are saying is just crazy."

"I'm about to lose my job."

"You can still umpire. They can't stop you because of one mistake."

"It's not just because I got caught in the play, it's because…"

"Once they realize there's nothing here," he waved his hand between the two of them. "They'll move on, and you'll get your place back. Surely."

"I don't know how I'm going to face the fellas at training again."

Zac looked at her, and saw something he hadn't seen ever before. He guessed now everyone had seen it, it would be hard going back.

"They've all suddenly seen you as a woman, Maddie, that's the problem. An attractive and probably desirable woman."

"Probably?"

"Definitely, but that's not something I should really be saying, considering our circumstances, is it?"

"Zac Beecham, we aren't team members anymore. You and I shouldn't be seeing each other, or be having anything to do with each other."

"I'll get on the phone to your dad, give him all the reports he needs, then I better disappear from your life, I think. That would be best."

Maddie nodded. She made another attempt to stand up, but over-balanced and fell back on the bed. Zac stepped over and took her hand, carefully helping her to stand up. He handed her the fallen crutches.

"You okay?" He locked eyes with her as he searched her face. There was a crazy electric moment when Zac felt as if he was fused to her. His hands were on her shoulders, and his eyes went to her lips.

"You have to leave, Zac."

The spell was broken. He stepped back, being careful not to upset her balance.

"I'm leaving, but first, I think I'll get you some breakfast, or you'll likely end up burning yourself with spilled coffee or something."

***

Zac left Maddie's apartment and was met by several reporters who jostled him for a comment.

"How is the ref this morning?"

"How long has your relationship been going?"

"Ms. Grace has been accused of a conflict of interest. Have you any comment?"

"Do you know there's to be an internal investigation into corruption?"

"Is Ms. Grace all right?"

This was the one question Zac was prepared to answer, so he zeroed in on the reporter who asked. "She's not all right, actually," Zac said. "Apart from the fact that she was injured in the incident, she is now being accused of something she didn't do, and is being submitted to a media frenzy. I think she would do much better if you just left her alone."

Zac turned from the pack of reporters and got into the taxi he'd ordered. He directed it to the stadium to pick up his car—and to see if he could get Maddie's bag and phone sent back to her place. The stadium security guard was happy to let him in to the umpires' locker room, and Zac had her combination number. He had hoped he might have got someone else to take the bag back to her, but there was only stadium staff there, and no one wanted to take responsibility. He got in his car and put his phone through Bluetooth, then called Jimmy Grace.

"You two have made a fine mess of things down there," Jimmy said the moment he answered the phone. "I don't think I've ever seen such a fuss."

"You've seen plenty of fuss before," Zac said. "How many times do the media follow players around because of drink-driving or drugs or partying or accusations of rape?"

"Sure enough, but they're loving your fall from grace, pardon the pun."

"Jimmy, you know that nothing has been going on, don't you?"

"That's what Maddie told me, and I haven't known her to lie."

"And she's not lying now. Look, I've got her sports bag and phone, and I'm about to drop it back to her apartment, but there are reporters everywhere. It's all got out of hand."

"So I saw in the paper."

"I'm thinking I might ask my sister to pop down and spend a couple of days with her. Maddie's struggling and shouldn't be on her own in my opinion. I'd stay, but that would only make this media storm worse."

"Do you think I should come down?" Jimmy asked.

"When I drop her phone back, you can talk to her about it, but I'll ask Ali if she can help out. She loves an opportunity to come to Melbourne, so will probably jump at the chance."

"Okay. Zac…" Jimmy paused.

"Yeah?"

"There had better not be anything in what I'm reading."

Zac was taken aback. "What do you mean?"

"Knocked out, then knocked up."

"Good grief! That's a headline? I hope Maddie doesn't see it."

"Not a headline. That's what Ted Hills says is the joke around her colleagues. Personally I want to knock some heads together, and I'm hoping yours is not one of them."

Zac swallowed.

"Zac?" Jimmy pounced on his hesitation.

"I haven't done anything with your daughter other than look after her last night, but I need to say…"

"Need to say what, Zac?"

"She's not one of the boys, Jimmy. She's an attractive woman, and I've got eyes in my head."

"What are you saying?"

"I'm just saying, I don't feel like her mate or her brother."

"Have you told her that?"

"At this stage, I'm making a quick getaway for both our sakes."

"You better treat her with respect, Zac Beecham, or you'll have me to answer to."

"You have my word."

***

Maddie couldn't believe the crowd of reporters camped outside her apartment. She didn't even dare go outside—not after she'd watched Zac fight his way through with her sports bag and phone. He'd tried to ignore them, but cameras were filming and flashing, and just once he stopped and said something. She hoped it wasn't something that would appear as yet another headline. *These people are crazy.* They smelled blood and wanted to tear Zac apart.

"I don't understand why this is such a big deal," Maddie said when he'd finally made it inside.

"It's because of my faith," Zac replied. "They don't want to believe that I'm genuine."

"Do you really think that's it? Why should they care?"

"Do you know what they just asked me?"

Maddie shook her head. She couldn't lip read.

"They want to know if you were my first."

"First…girlfriend?"

"First sexual experience."

Maddie tried to swallow, but her throat was dry. "That is so intrusive. And anyway, why should it matter to them?"

Zac sighed. "I did an interview a couple of years back, and they asked me about my faith. The whole sexual morality thing came up, and I told them what I believed."

"Which is?"

"Sex is between a man and woman in the sacred bounds of marriage."

Maddie wasn't surprised. She knew what Zac believed. She had the same views herself, but nobody cared what she believed.

"They challenged me on it then. Blew it out of proportion like as if I belong to some crazy misogynist cult, and they've been waiting to trip me up ever since."

"I'm sorry, Zac. I feel as if this is my fault."

"How is it your fault?"

Maddie shrugged. "What did you tell the reporters when you came in?"

"I told them to back off and leave you alone."

"Is that all?"

"If I said anything else, they'd twist it to suit their agenda."

"But did you deny that there was anything between us?"

"I've already said it several times earlier. Saying it again isn't going to make any difference, besides…"

"Besides what?" Maddie asked, alarmed.

"There is something between us now, isn't there?"

Maddie studied his face. "What do you mean?"

"We're obviously close enough for me to care about helping you. I feel awful about what happened, and responsible."

"There isn't much you can do, Zac. I mean, I appreciate your being here, getting my bag, making my breakfast and all."

"I know. I'm going, but am hoping you wouldn't mind if my sister, Ali, dropped in to help out for a bit."

"I don't know your sister."

"Doesn't matter. She's good value, and on her way to Melbourne as we speak."

"Where does she live?"

"Torquay—the surf coast where my parents live."

"I feel a bit funny relying on someone I don't know."

"Do you have another friend in Melbourne you'd feel more comfortable asking?"

Maddie shook her head. "Only other guys, and they'll be training for the finals, not wanting to be playing nursemaid."

"You'll get on fine with Ali. She won't take any rubbish from those journos."

Chapter Five

Maddie was relieved to find that Zac was right. Ali was good value. She was friendly, caring, chatty, and she gave the pack of reporters an earful the minute she arrived. That didn't make any difference. There were still a few camped outside, obviously waiting for Zac to return.

"So how long have you and my brother been friends?" Ali asked, once she'd made lunch and had the apartment in good order.

"Don't you start," Maddie replied.

"Well, you are obviously friends, or he wouldn't have got involved helping you out."

"He was in my dad's team a few years ago. I was part of the support staff. I knew him from then."

"Did you go out together?"

"Are you kidding? Dad would have killed any of his players who treated me like…"

"Like a girl?"

"I was one of the boys, and they all knew the rules, including Zac."

"But you're not one of the boys."

"I am when it comes to football."

"Did you see the photo of you and Zac in the morning paper?"

"I've been trying to avoid media."

"It's cute. You'll like it."

Ali opened her tablet and scrolled through. "Here. What does that look like to you?"

Maddie's feelings began to war inside her. One part was alarmed, the other part went all warm and fuzzy. Ali had opened to a series of pictures taken as they were leaving the hospital. She was balanced on crutches wearing Zac's colorful football guernsey. It looked good on her as a miniskirt, showing her shapely legs. The next shot showed Zac pulling his fleecy hoodie over his head, and the third shot showed him helping her adjust it, so she was warm.

"Cute, isn't it?" Ali said.

"What am I supposed to say?" Maddie asked.

"I've never seen him like that before," Ali said. "I think he likes you."

"I think you're letting the media influence your imagination."

"Would it be so bad if he did?"

"I could lose my job because of a supposed relationship with him, and they're accusing me of a conflict of interest."

"Mmm." Ali sat back in the lounge chair and took a sip of her herbal tea. "That's not good for you, is it?"

"No. And not only that, the media seemed obsessed with your brother's sex life—whether he has one or not."

"Yeah, I know. He's usually more careful about that."

"So I'm not sure cute is that great a development at the moment."

"You're probably right. Listen…" Ali suddenly sat forward in her chair and put her tea cup on the coffee table. "What say you come back to Torquay with me for a while? Let's give your ankle time to heal away from this crazy bunch." She waved her hand towards the window outside which the paparazzi were camped.

"I hate to impose."

"You're one of Zac's friends. My mother will love having you, and I'll try my best not to let my imagination get carried away."

Maddie looked at her swollen foot propped up on a kitchen chair. It was black and blue, and about the size of an elephant's foot. She couldn't manage on her own. Her grandparents in Perth weren't able to travel and her dad needed to stay in Brisbane to get his team ready for the finals. This was a good invitation, and Ali was good value.

"If you're sure it's not too much trouble."

"No trouble at all," Ali said as she got up and took the tea cups over to the sink.

***

Zac's family was lovely. Ali was fun and talked about her brother all the time. Maddie got the feeling Ali was trying to encourage Maddie to seriously think about him. She could hardly not think about him. Zac's father was about Zac's size and stature and was obviously where Zac got his good looks from. Zac's mother was kind, caring and outwardly Christian, like Zac. When Ali drove her through Torquay to the coffee shop, there was a billboard on the side of the road with Zac's picture on it, promoting some sort of fancy watch. He was everywhere, but nowhere to be seen.

Maddie hadn't been a regular churchgoer since her mother passed away. But she had a faith that had been inspired by her grandparents. Now, while at the Beecham's house, she was a regular churchgoer. Three times a week, in fact. She didn't mind. She didn't have training to go to, and it was nice to be reminded of the legacy of faith her mother had left her. Not only that, but the Beecham's church had a warm family atmosphere.

"So this is Zac's girl?" A friendly woman approached Maddie the first time she set her foot inside the church building. "You're a lot taller than you look in the pictures."

"That's because she is always standing next to Zac in the pictures," Ali said. "He's six foot five."

"How tall are you, dear?" the woman asked.

Maddie wanted to laugh. What an odd way to introduce yourself. "Nearly 176 centimeters."

"Imperial measurements, dear. I never did convert."

"I think about five foot nine."

"Perfect. That's what Zac needs—a woman who isn't too short."

Maddie turned a look to Ali and frowned. Ali just laughed.

"Aren't you going to help me out here?" Maddie whispered.

"The church already love you," Ali whispered back. "They think they own Zac, so they're just making sure you're the right fit for him."

"I thought we'd discussed this. You promised you wouldn't let your imagination get carried away."

"Just go with it. It's not hurting anyone to let folks have their fun with the idea of romance."

"Except Zac and me."

"Would you be so opposed to the idea of considering Zac for real?"

"Being as you're on about it like every five minutes, I don't have much choice but to consider it."

Ali turned a deadpan face towards Maddie, and raised her eyebrows. "So what's the problem?"

Maddie wanted to burst out laughing, except that the congregation was settling down ready for the service to begin. "What about Zac? How do you suppose he'll feel having his family and church friends organizing his love life?"

"He will laugh, pat us condescendingly on the head and ignore us." Ali turned to face the front of the church.

"Yes, but what if I take it seriously, and then get massively crushed with disappointment when he laughs at the idea?"

"Are you taking it seriously?" Ali turned back to face Maddie. The look of hope on her face was priceless.

"You were the one who said it was cute. You keep suggesting it. He is a very good looking, perfectly formed unit. Since there isn't a football or whistle involved, I haven't been keeping my professional guard up."

"You wait til I tell him what you've said."

"Ali!"

"Shh!" Ali put her finger to her lips and motioned with her eyes forward. The church service had started.

What have I got myself into?

Maddie thought the discussion was over, but Ali took it up again in the car on the way home.

"Zac asks after you every time he calls."

Maddie rolled her eyes. "Ali—"

"And you should know he's been calling every day."

"Doesn't he always?"

"Call every day? Not likely. We're usually lucky to hear from him once a fortnight."

"That doesn't mean anything, does it?" A crazy jolt of something shot through Maddie's veins. Was it hope? What was she hoping for?

"He only asks after you," Ali said.

"He's concerned because of the accident." The excuse sounded lame.

"You think?"

"If it was anything else, he would have called me, wouldn't he?"

Ali laughed.

"You really are hopeless," Maddie said.

"Can I ask you something?" Ali turned serious.

"Sure."

"How serious are you about your faith?"

"Honestly?"

Ali nodded.

"When Mum died, I figured Dad must have blamed God. I vaguely remember going to church as a family, but not after Mum died. Dad doesn't talk about God or faith. It's all football for him."

"What about you?"

"Dad has been my major influence since I was three, but my grandparents still talked to me about God and faith. Even though they lost their daughter, they encouraged me to know and love God."

"How does that look?"

"I guess I haven't been in the habit of going to church much. There is so much Sunday sport, and it is often a work day for me. But, when I'm in Perth, I always go to church with my grandparents."

"You know Zac hopes to work in Christian youth ministry."

"What, you mean like a pastor?"

"Maybe, or a Christian youth worker at least."

Maddie went quiet for moment.

"Would that bother you?" Ali asked.

"Why should it bother me?"

"If you marry him."

Maddie laughed out loud and slapped Ali's arm. "I'm not going to marry Zac," she said.

"Are you sure?"

Maddie shook her head. "You're incorrigible!"

"Such a big word."

"If your brother is mad enough to get involved with an umpire, threatening his reputation in the process—"

"And if said umpire returns the interest?"

"Faith is important to me, Ali. Perhaps it's time for me to give it more priority in my life."

They had pulled into the driveway in front of Ali's parent's house. She switched off the ignition and turned to Maddie, grinning.

"Well that's great news, Maddie Grace. I can see this working out perfectly."

***

Zac's football season had ended with the beginning of finals. His team mates were planning the usual overseas football trip which would feature a lot of drinking and hooking up with whatever women were up for a party. He didn't want to go, but hated the idea that they thought he was too good for them. In the end, he pleaded pain as the excuse for not going. The cracked ribs were, in all truth, still painful. He would've liked to head home to Torquay for his break, but knew that Maddie was there with his folks.

So he stayed on in his Melbourne apartment. Then his mother called.

"Why don't you come home until your pre-season training starts?" she asked.

"I thought the house might be a bit crowded."

"We do have four bedrooms, Zac. Yours is still free."

Zac took a deep breath and then decided to speak openly.

"Ali told me you guys have all been pairing me up with Maddie."

"I think the newspapers did that."

"Yes, but you're all encouraging it along."

"Don't you like her?"

Zac paused. He'd thought about it, of course. A bit hard not to since their supposed relationship had been a major feature on his social media.

"What does that pause mean?" his mother asked.

"It means I haven't really thought about it."

"Which is a lie!"

She always knows.

"I'm not sure it's a wise move at this stage." Zac twirled the draw-string of his jacket between his fingers.

"Why?"

"Because of the conflict of interest with our careers."

"Is that all?"

"It's sort of a major thing, Mum."

"What, so you're going to wait until you're thirty-something, and too old to play football before you consider forming a permanent relationship?"

"I don't have any mad rush to run out and find a wife. There are girls throwing themselves at me all the time. It won't be too hard when the time is right."

"You don't want one of those silly fan girls, Zac. You want someone who shares your passions and interests. Who is level-headed and sensible."

"Anything else on your list?" He knew he sounded a little bit sarcastic.

"I think you should come down to Torquay and spend some time with Maddie. Perhaps your on-field collision was not just an accident."

Zac finished the call. His mother could be so insightful and provoking it was almost infuriating. She was right, of course. As always.

Chapter Six

"Hi!"

Maddie jumped when Zac stepped into the spot next to hers at church. She hadn't been expecting him, but she guessed the rest of the family knew he was coming by the grin on Ali's face. She smiled up at him—the service had started, and she didn't feel it was appropriate to talk. But she was hyper-aware of him standing next to her as they joined in the hymn. After two weeks she was still on crutches, but improved enough to stand up while the congregation sang. She couldn't help but notice how she compared to him in height. *Perfect.* Just like half the women in the congregation had said. They were probably sitting in their pews taking mental note and getting ready to add more affirmation to the 'get-Maddie-and-Zac-together' campaign they seemed to have organized.

"How is your foot?" Zac asked her the moment the service was over.

"It's being remarkably slow to heal," Maddie said.

"Are they sure it's not broken?"

"I went to the local GP, and he didn't seem too concerned. I guess I just have to wait. There was no hope of me umpiring in the finals anyway."

"I thought I'd come home for a couple of weeks before the Medal Count Gala Dinner. Hope you don't mind."

"Did you bring your journo friends with you?"

"Hardly friends. More like pesky flies."

Maddie laughed. "Did you bring the flyspray?"

"Afraid not. Since the...incident...they always seem to know where I am."

Maddie looked around the church.

"There's a couple of paparazzi parked outside. They'll probably follow me home."

"But what if they see me?"

"They already know you're here. Haven't you been paying attention to social media?"

Maddie shook her head. "What are you going to do?"

Zac shrugged. "Not much I can do. We just need to play it cool, and hopefully you can keep up a busy social schedule with Ali."

"You do know that your family and friends have other ideas. Playing it cool is not one of the options."

"I know."

Maddie saw Zac look around the church auditorium to see who was watching. Almost everybody. She realized Zac was used to being in the spotlight. He was recognized everywhere, a by-product of being considered one of Australia's top players, a contender for the Best and Fairest Medal, and loved by advertising agencies. Ali had told her about the folks in his hometown who knew him before he got famous. They felt as if they had their own interest in him, but they would also protect him if it came to it. Then he did something that surprised Maddie.

"Pete, could you close the main doors and keep any strangers out," Zac called to the head usher. "I have a closed announcement I'd like to make."

"What are you doing?" Maddie asked, alarmed.

"Clearing the air."

Everyone gathered to where Zac stood with Maddie, and Maddie wondered if she might die of embarrassment.

"It's no use pretending you guys haven't heard all the media fuss that's been going on."

"Riveting viewing," an older lady said. "Can't wait to watch the talk shows."

"Well, here are the facts," Zac said. "Maddie and I used to be teammates in my last team. She was support staff, and I was a junior player. Her dad was my coach. We haven't seen each other since I left that team. We didn't have any relationship other than teammates. The recent on-field collision was the first time I've seen Maddie in several years. The media have made a mountain out of nothing."

"That's a shame," another lady said. "You look good together."

"The thing is," Zac continued, "Maddie and I could be good friends, but these stories are hurting her professional career. She needs the opportunity to umpire at the elite level, just as much as I want to play at the elite level. If we have any sort of relationship, she loses her chance."

"That's not fair," Ali said. "Why don't they drop you instead?"

Zac frowned at his sister. Ali shrugged her shoulders. "So much for equal opportunity," she said under her breath.

"Anyway," Zac continued, "can you guys keep your speculation down to a dull roar? Maddie and I have enough of a friendship from the past that we might catch a coffee together, or go for a walk on the beach without everybody making crazy comments, or posting pictures on the net. Okay?"

"Fine with us." Zac's mother decided to speak on behalf of the church crowd. "All right with you?" She directed the question around the room.

There was a general mumble of agreement.

"Because, if you don't support us, Maddie will be on the first plane to Perth before she's had a chance to recover." Zac looked to Maddie. "Do you have anything to add?"

"Thanks for your hospitality." Maddie gave a weak smile that she felt was anything but adequate.

The congregation broke up and began to move outside.

"I'll see you at home later," Zac said to her. He gave her a warm smile and Maddie melted on the inside as she watched him walk out of the church.

"He's mad about you," Ali said in her ear as he left. "Pfft! Friends! How stupid does he think we are?"

Maddie tried to form her best stern, disapproving look and cast it towards Ali, who just laughed in return.

"I'm not buying it, Maddie Grace. You're mad about him too, aren't you?"

***

The spring weather was moody. There were patches of beautiful sunny skies, but then the weather turned grey and windy.

"It's good surfing weather," Zac said to Maddie over the breakfast table.

"Do you surf?"

"Not at the moment." He pointed to his injured ribs.

"We've lived here since the kids were born," Rod Beecham said over his coffee cup. "We're two hundred meters from one of the world's best surf beaches. What sort of parent would I be if I didn't teach them to surf?"

"Do you surf, Maddie?" Nina Beecham asked.

Maddie shook her head. "My childhood was football, football, football."

"Hence a career in football," Zac said.

"You could teach her to surf," Ali said.

"Not at the moment." Zac and Maddie answered at the same time, and everybody laughed.

"Why don't you kids go for a walk on the beach today?" Nina asked. Maddie knew she was scheming.

"I still need the crutches," Maddie said. "They'd sink in the sand, and I wouldn't make it ten meters."

"Zac could give you a piggy back."

"Ali, honestly! You are so not being subtle. I thought we agreed not to make something of this." Maddie was surprised at her own confidence.

"I couldn't anyway," Zac said. He pointed to his ribs a second time.

"Right." Maddie sipped her coffee.

"But we could go and sit on the beach and watch waves for a while, if you like?"

Maddie was surprised that this suggestion came from Zac. She looked to Ali, and it wasn't hard to lip read her smart-alec comment. *I told you.*

"Sure. Why not." Yes. Maddie wanted to sit on the beach with Zac. Wanted to talk to him. Wanted to find out exactly what was going on inside his head.

The wind still had a bite in it, so Maddie dressed warmly. The Beecham's house had to be worth a load of money situated where it was, right on the beachfront. She knew she could make the short distance to the sand using her crutches. Ali started out with them, as agreed, but the moment they'd found a nice spot on the sand to watch the surfers, Ali suddenly remembered she'd forgotten her mobile phone.

"That's convenient," Maddie mumbled as she watched Ali head back toward the house. "What do you bet she takes forever to come back?"

"Maddie."

Maddie heard a serious tone in Zac's voice, and turned to look at him.

"Are you okay?" she asked.

"Yeah, I'm good. I thought we should talk about…" He waved his hand between them.

"I thought you were going to disappear from my life."

"Well, if that's what you want. Once your foot is better, that can be the last of it."

"I like you, Zac."

"Like?"

"Like. You're kind, funny, caring, not to mention incredibly good-looking and hot." She looked at the beach, out to sea, anywhere but at him.

"Hot?" He nudged her with his elbow and waited. She could tell he was looking right at her. She swung her gaze back to face him. He was grinning.

"Cut it out. You know you're hot. You have all those fan girls gagging over you."

"Yeah, but to have a mature, intelligent and beautiful woman say it makes all the difference."

"Zac. We're flirting. Is this helpful?"

"Depends on what we're hoping to achieve."

"I like it, for the moment, but for the long term, you know what it means for me and my career."

Zac nodded.

"Aren't you going to ask me why my career is so important to me?"

"I don't have to ask. I know. It's like my career. It's your life and all you've worked towards."

Maddie felt an incredible wave of something good flow over her. He understood. He didn't even question it.

"If I was to consider giving up my career, I'd need to know what for. It would have to be something so much better."

"I get it," Zac said.

Maddie waited for more, but Zac just stared out towards the ocean and the surfers catching waves.

"Is that the end of the discussion?" she asked.

"Do you want to come with me to the Medal Dinner?"

That was the last question she'd expected.

"Who do you usually take?" she asked.

"Mum or Ali."

Maddie smiled.

"Well?" He raised his eyebrows in question.

"I better not, Zac."

"Right, because of the media, and your career."

"And also I'm Dad's date. I've been with him every year since I was eighteen."

Zac nodded, and fell silent again.

"Besides, Ali would love the chance to glam up again, if I read her right."

"Yeah, she likes the opportunity to get the full treatment, especially since I pay for it."

"Do you?" Maddie smiled. "You're a nice brother."

"She couldn't afford to on the amount she earns, and given the amount we professional footy players earn, well…"

"And it is also your public image too, on the red carpet."

The conversation stilled again.

"I'll go back to Melbourne once I'm back on two feet," Maddie said. "After the Medal Dinner, I'll probably go back to Perth until after Christmas.

Zac nodded.

"Thanks for helping me out, and letting me stay with your family."

"They've loved having you," Zac said. "Besides, they have an ulterior motive."

"They're trying to get us together for real."

"You've noticed."

"They're not very subtle."

Zac smiled.

"Well, I'll give them the stern talk when we get back."

"What will you tell them?"

"To back off and leave you alone. You can't even consider a relationship with the likes of me if you hope to earn your place back umpiring the seniors."

Maddie nodded. That was what she'd told him. She didn't tell him that right now her place umpiring senior competition was nowhere near as attractive as he was. But that might just be the fact that she was sitting so close to him that their shoulders touched, and there was some strange sort of warm current passing between them. She should move away from him, but the current seemed to have dulled her good sense. And when he put his arm around her shoulder and she fit snugly against his side, her good sense disappeared altogether.

***

"You guys are so cute together." Ali didn't even try to hide her thoughts. "I wish you'd just get over your issues and make it official."

"Not gonna happen, sis," Zac said. "Maddie's career is important to her, and I'm not going to be the one to stuff it up."

"I think you've already stuffed it up." Ali laughed. "But if you want to go through the exercise..." She shrugged her shoulders.

"So are you going to go to the Medal Dinner with him?" Ali asked Maddie.

"Can't let my dad down," Maddie replied. "He's my standing date."

"Oh." Her disappointment was obvious. "Then perhaps we can double date."

"Jimmy and Maddie will be with their team; you and I will be sitting with my team." Zac rolled his eyes, as if his sister should know better.

"Then you're going to take me again?" Ali asked.

"Perhaps you can use the dress you bought last year, and get my money's worth out of it."

"Zachary Beecham. You know full well that the cameras and commentators will make special note of what I wear, and they'll never let you live it down if it's a rerun from last year."

"Might take the heat off Maddie for a bit."

Maddie smiled. The commentators had never really cared what she wore. Jimmy Grace was a respected coach, but he wasn't the media favorite like Zac was. The whole red-carpet spectacle was a bit over the top for her. She usually played it down a bit—made the effort to look nice, but didn't play the provocative card with backless dresses or necklines that ended at her navel.

"Hey, Maddie, since my brother is paying the bill, do you want to come shopping together for formal gowns, shoes and stuff? Then we could go to the spa together, and get our hair and nails done. You know, the works."

"He's not paying for me," Maddie said.

"Can't you afford the whole works?" Ali asked.

"I can. We umpires get paid well too. I'd love to do the glam girl thing with you, if you like."

"Great. That's settled then. My work here is done." She got up to go back to the house.

"Wait for me," Maddie said. "I'll come with you."

Zac stood up to help Maddie get upright and balanced on her crutches.

"I hope you can get your foot into some heels by Medal night," he said. "It's only two weeks away."

"I can wear flats. It doesn't bother me."

Zac smiled. He walked with them back to the house. Far from having cleared things up during their talk on the beach, she was now more confused than ever. Zac Beecham had landed back in her life, and she couldn't seem to dislodge him.

Even if she'd wanted to.

Which she didn't.

Chapter Seven

Maddie had been back in her apartment for a full three days when Ali called and arranged to come and stay over for a shopping trip. Shops and fashion weren't Maddie's thing, but Ali was in her element and her enthusiasm was infectious. She'd already done her research online so they didn't have to walk miles. Instead she'd chosen a few boutique stores that had what they were looking for. Ali tried to push Maddie into being a bit more daring than usual, but Maddie resisted. She couldn't help but think about Zac and how his "good Christian boy" image might be affected if she dressed too provocatively. Wait! She wasn't going with Zac. But Dad would wonder what on earth she was doing if she started showing flesh.

"Well, it's a change from your sports shorts and umpires top," Ali said. "I don't think the commentators will recognize you."

"Hopefully not. I'd like to keep out of their line of sight for a while."

"Is it okay if I stay over for a couple of days in Melbourne? I have a few things I'd like to get done in the city, and then on the day of the Medal Count, we can go to the spa together. Is that still all right?"

"That's fine," Maddie answered.

"My dad is arriving on the day of the dinner, but you'll go home with Zac after the dinner, won't you?"

Ali nodded. "I wish you were going with him," she said.

"Then you'd miss out on going. You want to go, don't you?"

"Yeah, but I think I'd like it more to see him happy."

"He's happy, isn't he?"

"No. He's like a lost puppy. I've never seen him like this. He's got it bad for you, but he won't stand in the way of your career."

"Ali, did he tell you that, or is this just more of your hopeful imagination?"

"He didn't have to tell me. I can read him."

Maddie shook her head and rolled her eyes. "You should write romance novels. I don't think they'd be any more unbelievable than what you come up with here."

"You can protest all you like. I know my brother."

***

Maddie enjoyed Ali's larger-than-life personality. She brought energy to Maddie's apartment that was missing when she was alone. The prospect of going to the Medal Dinner with her dad wasn't usually such a highlight, but with Ali's presence, it was something different. Beauty spas and manicures weren't something Maddie did usually, but she was having fun this time. But when she walked back into her apartment, hair coiffed and nails glistening, she was arrested by the sight of her father…and another woman.

"Hi Dad." She knew she sounded uncertain.

"Wow, you look gorgeous," he said.

"It's the Medal Dinner. There are red-carpet obligations."

Jimmy laughed. He stepped around Maddie and held his hand out towards Ali. "Hi, I'm Jimmy, Maddie's father."

"Oh, this is Ali," Maddie said. "We've been shopping and getting ready for tonight."

"And this is Ellen," Jimmy said.

"Hi." Maddie knew her voice sounded high-pitched and uncertain. *Who was Ellen?*

"Ah, I'll just pop in to the kitchen and make some coffee," Ali said. "You guys might want a minute."

"Actually, let us make the coffee," Jimmy said. "I just need to catch up with my daughter for a bit. We won't be long."

Maddie had a funny feeling that she wasn't going to like what he had to say, but she followed her father into the small kitchenette.

"Who's Ellen?" she asked, once she'd closed the door.

"My fiancée."

"What?" Maddie couldn't help the aggression in her voice. She'd had no idea her father had been seeing someone. They had been a pair since she was three years old, and there had never been talk of anyone else.

"I'm sorry, Maddie. I should have warned you."

"Yes, you should have."

"I just thought that you were so caught up with Zac and all that, I didn't want to throw this at you over the phone."

Maddie didn't say anything. There was too much to process.

"I've been seeing Ellen for a while, but didn't consider getting serious until I saw you and Zac were together, and I thought that maybe it might be time for me to consider my own life for once."

"Zac and I are not together."

"Really? The media still have you pegged as a couple."

"We're friends, that's all."

"No chance of anything more?"

"Not with our careers clashing."

"You won't have your careers forever, Maddie. There's more to life than just sport."

"Really? You could have fooled me, from what I've seen of your life."

"Maddie, when your mother died, I threw myself into football because I didn't have anything else."

"You had me."

"And you loved football too."

Maddie couldn't deny that.

"But there comes a time when you realize there is more to life. You and I live in different cities. I come home from training to an empty apartment. You must feel the same, being here on your own."

Maddie nodded.

"I've gotten to know Ellen, and we get on well together. I've asked her to marry me, and I hope you'll give me your blessing."

"I'm sorry, Dad. It was just a shock. I didn't realize…"

"My fault. I should have warned you."

Maddie stepped into his open arms and enjoyed the closeness she'd always felt in her father's strong embrace.

"I love you, Maddie. And I'm hoping you'll find a strong relationship too, soon."

"Wait." Maddie pulled back and looked up into his face. "Are you taking Ellen to the Medal Dinner?"

Jimmy nodded.

"But I was going as your date, like we always have."

"I thought Zac was going to ask you."

"How did you know that?"

"He asked me if I'd mind."

"Really?"

"Aren't you going with him?"

"No, I told him I was going with you. Ali—his sister—is his date."

"Oh, that's a fine mess I've made of things, and you look so gorgeous, with your hair and makeup all done."

Maddie's heart dropped. "It's all right. I don't need to go. You can't let your fiancée down."

Jimmy hugged Maddie again. "I'm sorry."

Maddie pulled back again. "Wait. Where is she staying?"

"We were going to stay here." Jimmy raised his eyebrows in question.

"In the same room?"

Jimmy just pursed his lips.

"Dad, that's so…awkward. After what Zac and I have been through, it's a bit dodgy too."

"I don't have the same convictions about things as Zac does," Jimmy said.

"Yes, but I'm your daughter."

"Don't worry about it. I'll book us into a hotel."

Maddie's happy day had been dimmed by disappointment. Now she was all dressed up with nowhere to go, and to make matters worse, her dad was sleeping with a woman she didn't know. She much preferred Zac's ideal of waiting for marriage. She wouldn't say it out loud, but it did make her admire Zac just that bit more. As if she needed anything else to admire about him.

***

Zac walked in to Maddie's apartment to find Ali and Maddie in a full-blown disagreement.

"Hey, what's going on?"

"She won't get ready to go." Maddie pointed towards Ali.

"You're not ready either, I see," Zac said.

"I'm not going."

"Yes, you are," Ali said. "I don't need to go. You go with Zac."

"What's going on here?" Zac asked. Both women had their hair and makeup done, but neither was dressed for a gala dinner. And someone was missing. "Where's your dad?"

Maddie dropped her gaze and looked upset.

"Her dad turned up with another woman. Maddie doesn't have a date." Ali stood with her arms folded across her chest.

"She's his fiancée." Maddie sounded defensive.

"You still don't have a date, so I'm going to stay home and you can go with Zac." Ali was using the you'll-do-as-I-say-or-else tone Zac remembered from countless childhood arguments.

"Wait. What?" Zac was finding it hard to catch up.

"It's all right, Zac. I don't have to go. I'm happy to sit and watch the count on TV."

"I'm not going," Ali said. "I've got a headache, and I'm going to lie down."

"Would you two stop your arguing," Zac said, raising his voice a notch. "Let me get this straight. Your Dad got engaged and brought his fiancée as his partner for the dinner?"

Maddie nodded.

"And he didn't tell you before?"

"He thought I was going with you, and didn't want to tell me about Ellen over the phone."

"He totally screwed it up, is what," Ali said.

"He didn't mean to."

Zac could see that Maddie was upset. He decided to divert the attention away from her father.

"So without a date, you planned to stay home."

"That is the only option. I don't have an invitation of my own."

"But Ali has a headache, so she can't come with me."

"She doesn't have a headache."

"I do too." Ali began to pull bobby pins out of the pile of hair on her head. "I'm not going, Zac. If Maddie won't go with you, then you don't have a date either."

Maddie rolled her eyes.

"But what if Zac doesn't want to be manipulated into taking me to the dinner, Ali? Did you think of that?"

"Yeah, Ali." Zac turned a stern look at her, with eyebrows raised. "Did you think of how I would feel about being manipulated?"

"Don't be ridiculous," Ali said. "You wanted to take Maddie in the first place. Now you can, and I'm just as happy to sit here on the couch and watch you win your Best and Fairest Medal."

"I'm not tipped to win," Zac said.

"You're a contender," Maddie said. "Though I wouldn't put money on you."

"Thanks very much."

They all laughed, which lowered the tension a couple of notches.

"I couldn't bet on you anyway, as I'm one of the umpires, remember. Conflict of interest."

"And that is the bottom line, Maddie. If you go with me tonight, there will be questions raised all over the place again, especially when the votes for the medal have been cast by your professional colleagues."

"I cast votes too, you know."

Zac nodded.

"She's not coming with me, Ali. You better suit up, quick sticks, or we'll be late."

Ali looked chagrined. Zac knew she didn't like to be outsmarted.

"Hurry up," Zac said. "I paid for all this regalia. I better get some value for money."

Ali dragged herself into the spare bedroom muttering something about the stupidity of professional ethics.

"I wish you were coming with me, though," Zac said, after his sister left the room.

"You look gorgeous, even in your jeans and t-shirt."

"Thanks. But we both know it's better if I don't."

Zac nodded. "I'm sorry you're going to be here all on your own."

He watched and saw her eyes brighten again, the same as the day Ted had told her she'd been dropped from senior umpiring. Suddenly he didn't care, and stepped across and folded her in a hug. She rested her head on his shoulder and wrapped her arms around his waist. This closeness felt so good. So right.

"You look and smell so good, Zac," she said.

"Would you put your dress on so I can see what you would have looked like on the red carpet?"

"Yeah, go on," Ali said, as she entered the room with her high-heeled shoes in her hand. "I'd like to get a picture with us all together."

"It feels kind of pointless now," Maddie said.

"Please." Zac wouldn't let her go from his gaze.

She sighed and went into her bedroom. "I'll go and give her a hand," Ali said. "You guys would have looked great together."

Zac paced around the lounge area. He hated the fact that Maddie was left behind without a date, especially since she'd gone to the trouble of getting ready. But she was right. They couldn't go together. If she went with him, there would be another media backlash questioning the integrity of the count. Eventually, Maddie emerged from her bedroom, and the sight of her nearly knocked him over.

"Ali, you must have something you need to do in the bathroom," he said.

His sister gave him a mock salute and disappeared.

"You are gorgeous, Maddie Grace. This is such a rubbish situation that I can't have you as my date. I would be the proudest man at the dinner if you were with me."

"Thanks, Zac. It's nice of you to say so."

"It's not just flattery either. I'm sorry to say it, but your hi-viz umpires' shirt doesn't do you justice. This outfit tells a different story."

Maddie smiled. Zac crossed the room to her and took her in his arms again. This time he tipped her face up with his fingertips, and kissed her.

"Let the newspapers say what they like," he said. "Perhaps they do need to do an investigation." Then he kissed her again. Far from being offended or upset, he found Maddie kissing him back.

"Ok, time's up," Ali said loudly, as she walked back into the room. "And don't let me hear any more nonsense from you, Maddie, about conflict of interest. I'll go out with him tonight, but it is the last time, do you hear?"

Chapter Eight

It was a good thing Maddie had insisted she stay home. Even without her there, she listened to various commentators make speculation about the ethics of an official vote-casting umpire being in a relationship with one of the players. For once, the cameras and commentators focused on her father, asking him pointed questions about where she was. Ali looked glamorous on the red carpet, but the focus shifted quickly from her to Zac, and the commentators asked him about his relationship with "the ref". Zac played it cool, and tried to point out how great his sister looked, but they weren't interested.

After the dinner, no one came back to Maddie's apartment. Her father and Ellen had booked into a hotel, and Zac took Ali to stay back at his apartment. A wise decision, but left Maddie feeling alone and lonely.

Then at two o'clock in the morning her phone rang. She saw it was Zac.

"Congratulations," she said.

"I only came fourth overall."

"Fourth out of how many hundreds? It was a fantastic result."

"I didn't call to talk about me. I called to see if you're all right."

Maddie paused for a brief moment.

"Maddie? You okay?"

"I'm a bit lonely, if I'm honest," she replied.

"I wish I could come over, but…"

"But that would be a really bad idea. There's still one tenacious reporter camped outside, and besides—"

"Even without the reporter, it would be a bad idea." Zac said.

"Why?"

"Because you're a woman, and I'm a man, and all of a sudden I can't seem to forget that. Ali and her matchmaking friends must have put something in my food."

Maddie laughed.

"You might think it's funny, but quite suddenly, all I can think of is being with you."

"You have a very romantic way about you, Zac."

"Not really. I know I'm not romantic. I just want to be with you."

"You've said that twice now."

"Yes, well. Ali and I are going back to Torquay tomorrow until after the Grand Final on the weekend. Do you want to come with us?"

"I do." Maddie didn't even take a moment to consider the offer. She wanted to be with him too. "Zac?"

"Yeah."

"You'd better talk to your agent about what's going on. The media are going to figure it out shortly, and if you don't get to it first, they'll say whatever thing comes into their collective imagination."

"Let's talk about it tomorrow. We'll be over at your place first thing to pick you up."

"It's nearly three in the morning. What do you mean by first thing?"

"If I don't go to sleep, is six a.m. too early?"

"Yes. I'm hoping yet to get some sleep. Make it after ten."

"There's only so much tossing and turning I can do before I go out of my mind."

"You'll be fine. I'll see you tomorrow."

***

By the time Ali, Maddie and Zac arrived back at Nina and Rod's place, there was a pack of reporters outside. Maddie climbed out of the car, having ridden in the front with Zac. Cameras clicked and questions were thrown in their direction.

"Why weren't you at the Medal Dinner?"

"How do you account for your lying about your relationship?"

"Rev, do you think honesty and integrity are important in sport?"

"Were you waiting until after the count to reveal your relationship?"

Zac chose not to answer any questions, as they had discussed during the drive from Melbourne. Maddie wanted to scream at them and tell them to mind their own business, but knew that would be a counterproductive exercise. Maddie watched various emotions chase across Ali's face. She'd been submitted to a firm lecture from both Zac and Maddie during the ride down the Princes Highway. They hadn't formulated a press release statement yet, and had told Ali she needed to ignore the media until they had spoken to Max.

Nina ushered them inside and closed the door on the intrusive reporters.

"What have you done now?" she asked her son.

"I'm not sure yet. Give us a couple of hours alone, and I'll let you know."

"What does that mean?" Nina asked.

Zac just smiled.

"I'm intrigued."

"You and the whole stupid press world," Ali said, waving her hand towards the front door.

Zac threw his bag in his room, and took Maddie's from her hand and put it in the spare room.

"Come on," he said, taking her hand. "I'm going surfing. You want to come and watch."

"You're mad," Ali said. "They'll mob you the moment you walk out that front door."

"I'm not going out the front door," he said. "I've climbed the back fence before."

"You're going to make Maddie climb the back fence?"

Maddie looked between Ali and Zac, and worried about the plan.

"She'll be fine. She runs about dodging thirty-six strong, athletic men for a living. She'll be fine jumping a fence."

Maddie shrugged. "If you say so."

Before she knew it, Zac had his surfboard and board-shorts, threw a couple of towels at her and led the way out the laundry door. There was a drum up against the fence and he easily lifted her up to stand on it.

"Your ribs have improved, I see," she said.

He nodded, and threw his board and shorts over the fence. Then he placed two hands on top of a fence post, and vaulted over the top. Impressive. The fence was as tall as she was. He held his hands up to help Maddie climb over. With his hands around her waist she jumped safely into the back-neighbors' garden. Before he let go, he placed a kiss on the top of her head.

"Let's get out of here," he said.

"Let's." Maddie was overwhelmed by Zac's whirlwind actions. She hadn't quite caught up, even as they passed by the neighbor who was mowing his lawn. Zac waved.

"Just avoiding the paparazzi out the front," he called as they went past.

"Good luck," the neighbor called, and went back to his mowing.

Zac led Maddie on a back streets detour that took them almost a kilometer further up the beach from where they would normally have gone. She was glad her foot was so much improved, or she wouldn't have been able to keep up. He set the towels on the sand in a sheltered location.

"Close your eyes," he said. "I can't be bothered finding a loo to get changed."

Maddie didn't need to be asked twice. She hid her eyes, and heard the sound of Zac's jeans hitting the sand next to her.

"Okay. All safe now."

Maddie looked up at him. He was peeling his close-fitting t-shirt off and it landed on top of the discarded jeans.

"Don't you need sunscreen?" She was unable to take her eyes from his gorgeous sculpted chest and abdomen muscles.

"Probably, but I left the house in such a hurry, I forgot to bring some."

"I've got an emergency tube in my bag," she said. "Sit down, and I'll do your back for you."

Zac plonked down on his towel next to her, and turned his back towards her. Maddie found her mouth going completely dry as she squeezed sunscreen onto his broad shoulders and along his rippling back muscles.

"You okay back there?" Zac asked.

"Ha ha," Maddie said. "You can put it on your front yourself."

"Not enjoying the exercise? I know I am."

Not only were Maddie's hands warm, so was her face, and insides. She thought she might just explode.

"Zac, obviously something has changed between us. We need to talk about it."

"I know." He turned around and looked her in the eye. "But right at the moment, I'm going to go for a surf. I need to cool off."

"Yes, I think you do."

He wasn't talking about the weather.

***

So this was sexual tension. Zac had been attracted to girls before. There were plenty of girls trying to attract his attention, using all means, fair and foul. But he hadn't stopped to look for long. He'd had his moral beliefs, and had read enough youth counselling books to know how it all worked. Don't play with fire, and you're less likely to get burned. He'd managed to keep himself fairly aloof from any emotional and physical entanglements—until he'd run into Maddie. Perhaps his mother was right. Perhaps it wasn't just an accident. She had him in knots, and neither of them had been trying to get involved—the exact opposite. He knew it was unfair to ask her to rub sunscreen on his back, but he'd enjoyed it. And very much wanted to return the favor.

This water is so not cold enough.

He only stayed in the water for half an hour. She was sitting on the beach watching him, and he wasn't enjoying the waves the way he normally would. He wanted to talk. They needed to talk. It was time to talk.

He shook the water from his hair as he emerged from the water, and jogged up the beach with his surfboard under his arm.

"So…" He stuck the pointy end of the board in the sand to stand it upright.

"So…" Maddie replied.

"What's going on between us?" he asked.

"I'm not sure, but I think we'd better make up our minds."

"I'm thinking love and marriage."

Maddie laughed out loud.

"Do you think that's funny or impossible?"

"I think you're funny. Direct and to the point."

"I'm not good at indirect hedging and dodging the real issues."

"Okay. Since that's the way you like to communicate, let's lay the cards on the table."

"I'm not just attracted to you, Maddie. I'm crazy about you. I'm not quite sure how that happened. How do you feel about me?"

"I'm not sure I have quite the same amount of confidence to just say it outright, like you do."

"Do you like me?"

Maddie nodded.

"More than like?"

She nodded again.

"Do you want me?"

"And then some."

"What about your career?"

Maddie shook her head. "I don't know what to do. I've worked for this all my life, and now all of a sudden…my focus has shifted."

"Do you think the umpires' league will consider modifying your schedule to make sure you don't ever get any of my games?"

"They make sure I don't umpire any of Dad's games, so I can't see why they couldn't do the same for yours."

"That's if they believe last season was all aboveboard and don't want to punish you."

Maddie nodded her head.

"If we do get together," she asked, "how will you feel about me working with all those men?"

Zac paused to think.

"You know how you went all funny rubbing sunscreen on my back?"

"How do you know I went all funny?"

"You did though, didn't you?"

Maddie nodded.

"Have you ever reacted to any of the other guys you've worked with like that before?"

"Never. I don't even think about sex when I'm at work."

"So you were thinking about sex, just now."

"Cut it out, Zac. You know there's something crazy going on between us."

"I know. I guess I'd be a hypocrite if I suggested you leave your work because of us. I have all sorts of women hanging around actually trying to get my attention. How do you feel about that?"

Maddie smiled.

"What's so funny?"

"They've tried so hard to get you, and all I had to do was run into a pack of players and get knocked out."

"Maddie, I do worry about you running around on a football field. You're so small and delicate."

Maddie frowned and put one hand on her hip. "Zac Beecham! I'll have you know I'm five foot nine, that's tall for a woman, and I can't buy women's sports shoes as they don't make my size. I have to buy men's sports shoes. And just look at how big my hands are."

She held up her hand to measure against his, but his extra-large hand dwarfed hers. Then she stopped talking, and he folded his fingers and wove them between hers. He brought their joined hands to his mouth and kissed her knuckles. He could feel her melting, and he didn't resist it. He put his arm around her shoulders and pulled her closer. She slipped her arm around his waist, and allowed her body to mould with his. Zac could feel the passion rush through his veins, and sensed it in Maddie as well. He didn't have to look for her lips, she offered them to him, full, soft and oh so kissable. Zac's heart nearly hammered out of his chest as Maddie's hand's explored his shoulders and arms.

"What do you think about love and marriage now?" His breathing was nearly as fast as his heart rate.

"Is that a proposal?" she asked.

He kissed her again without answering.

"I'll take that as a yes," she said.

"Please do. Will you marry me?"

"What about this afternoon?" Maddie said, then kissed him again.

***

Maddie was so high on love she didn't care about the reporters who weren't even trying to hide. There were telephoto lenses pointed in their direction. By this time, there were also a few beachgoers who had their phones out taking celeb photos. Zac Beecham was making out with his girlfriend on the beach. That was too good an opportunity to pass up.

But it was the phone call to Zac's agent, Max, that was really amusing.

"I told you I'd let you know if there were any developments," Zac said.

Maddie could hear a raised voice coming through on the other end of the line, but couldn't make out the words.

"I've just texted you two very cute selfies. You can sell them to whoever you like, but if I were you, I'd hurry, as the story will be out there in a very short time. There are no end of interested photographers here on the beach."

More raised tones, and Maddie thought she identified a couple of swear words.

"I'm not going to hide away, Max. Maddie and I are engaged… No, we were not involved at all before the accident…No, Maddie and I have never been involved in any way before…Yes, the accident was what brought us together…No, there has been no conflict of interest, no corruption…We'll have to see what Maddie's boss says about her umpiring career next season…This is what I pay you for, Max. It's your job to spin it in such a way that we come out looking good…Okay. I'll tell her."

Zac ended the call and grinned at her. "Max says congratulations."

"What have we done?" Maddie asked.

"We just got engaged to be married. I better call your dad before the media announces it."

"Good luck with that."

"Your dad will be happy as Larry. He already told me he hoped it would work out."

"Did he? He never said anything to me."

"I guess he didn't want to push you into something you didn't want."

"Oh, I want it," Maddie said. "You're like a drug, Zac Beecham. I don't know how I'm going to survive without you for the next couple of months."

Zac frowned at her. "I'm not going anywhere," he said.

"No, but I have to go home to Perth for a while."

"Do you have to?" He sounded like a whining child.

"I haven't seen my grandparents all year. They're the only family I have, apart from Dad. I need to spend some time with them."

"Can I come?"

Maddie grinned. "For a while, but your pre-season training will start, and your coach won't want you missing any of that."

Zac took her in his arms again, and she rested her head against his chest. It felt so good.

"We should probably go back to your folks place and put them out of their misery."

"What misery? They won't want us back until they're sure it's all sealed and delivered."

"You think they'll be happy about the engagement?"

"What do you think they've been hinting at the whole time?"

Maddie laughed. "Okay, then, let's go and give them the good news."

The next morning's headline:

NO CORRUPTION: The Rev falls for the Ref

Chapter Nine

Maddie spent some much-needed time with her aging grandparents, but Zac had been able to stay for only a few days. She missed him terribly after he left. There was a three-hour time difference between Perth and Melbourne, so they had a bit of trouble connecting on Skype. But that was all over now as she was back in Torquay for the Christmas break—and to pull off a secret wedding. The newspapers had lost interest in them now they were a respectable engaged couple. Only a couple of fashion mags still wanted to follow their story. Maddie wasn't sure if they liked the happy-ever-after romance aspect, or if they were hoping to find that one of them was cheating on the other, and were waiting for an ugly break-up. Those always made for a good cover.

Rod, Nina and Ali were the best support Maddie could have hoped for.

"Okay, so with this early-morning working bee…what's our cover story?" Ali asked.

"We're helping set up for the community Carols by Candlelight." Nina frowned at her daughter. "Dad and I always help."

"But this is the first year that you've decided to string fairy lights in all the trees surrounding the park. That looks suspicious to me."

"That's only because you know about the wedding. Nobody else will be any the wiser."

Maddie smiled as she watched the banter between her soon-to-be mother- and sister-in-law.

"It's Christmas Eve, Ali," Zac said. "There will be heaps of people out early to help set the park up for the carols."

"Do you usually help?" Ali asked her brother.

"I have in the past."

"That was before you became a superstar."

"What's your problem, Ali? I don't understand why you're so tense."

"We're supposed to be arranging a wedding, and all you have planned are fairy lights. I had much more in my mind by way of decorations, clothes, cars, pink swans—"

Maddie laughed outright.

"This will be perfect, Ali," she said.

"He earns gazillions." Ali looked accusingly at her brother. "And the cheapskate has opted for a tacked-on bonus at the end of Carols by Candlelight."

"It's not about money, Ali," Zac said.

"What's it about then?" she asked.

"It's about Maddie and me being happy."

"Are you happy, Maddie?" Ali swung her gaze and focused on her. "Deliriously."

"But, barefoot on the sand—and late at night. Really? Couldn't we have done better than that?"

Maddie stepped close to Zac and he put his arms around her.

"It is going to be perfect," Maddie said. "Now let's get these fairy lights up before the heat becomes unbearable."

It was forecast for a humid thirty-five degrees. There was some worry of a thunder storm later, but they were all hoping if one rolled through, it would be gone by the time the community Christmas event was due to start.

The day was warm, even at seven in the morning. By the time the Beecham family had wrestled with ladders and fought the frustration of tangled fairy-lights for a few hours, they were hot and glad they'd started early. Zac had been stopped a couple of times by kids who had approached him for an autograph. He was always friendly, and autographed whatever they had for him to sign.

"Are you going to come to the Carols tonight?" a pre-teen girl asked.

"For a while," Zac answered.

"Will you be singing?"

Zac laughed. "Singing is not my gift," he said. "I think we'll leave that to the professional musicians."

"Are you that lady umpire?" Her brother, about eight, pointed at Maddie.

Maddie nodded.

"Are you going to marry her?" he asked Zac.

"I think I will." Zac smiled at the boy and handed his signed T-shirt back to him.

"When?"

"Pretty soon." Zac stepped close to Maddie and put his arm around her. "Do you think that's a good idea?"

"Wait 'til I tell my dad." The boy rushed off full of enthusiasm to report his good fortune in uncovering the information.

"Pretty soon?" Maddie asked quietly.

"Twelve hours and counting."

"I'll go home and get some lunch," Nina said once they were satisfied they'd done their job. "Dad's going to stay on and help the team who are setting up the stage for tonight. What are you others going to do now?"

"She should be coming to the beauty salon," Ali said, pointing to Maddie. "We don't want to look like we've just washed up on the beach for this wedding."

"I'm only going to say this one more time, Ali," Maddie said. "Your hairdressing friend is dropping around later this afternoon, and that will be enough. Right now, I'm going to go back to your place and relax. Are you coming?" she asked Zac.

"I'm going to go for my last surf as a single man." He kissed Maddie. "I won't be long."

***

Zac loved the way he felt when he surfed. Relaxed and close to God. He had spent many occasions praying while he negotiated waves. Today was no different. He thanked God for the accident that had brought Maddie and him together. And he prayed he would be a good husband. It would not be without challenges. The media had left them alone for a while, but he had no doubt they would scrutinize his every move, and anything that looked dodgy they'd report on first and find out about later. He prayed that God would give him strength and wisdom, and that they would be able to face the pressures of a high-profile life without crumbling.

By the time he got back to his parents' house he found Maddie ready to relax on the couch.

"I'm going to watch one of the obligatory Christmas movies," she said. "Then we can get ourselves ready for this wedding."

"What are you going to watch?" Zac asked.

"*A Christmas Carol* or *Miracle on 34th Street*."

Zac flopped down on the couch next to her. It had reached the forecast temperature, and the air conditioner was working flat out. They were dressed in sleeveless tank tops and shorts.

"Got to have the snow and crackling fires to make it Christmas," Zac said. "I'd really get into the idea of all the warm drinks and woollen Christmas knits if it wasn't so hot."

"I see your mother has sprayed the fake frost on the window panes, and Bing Crosby was singing *White Christmas* during lunch.

"One of these years we'll have to go to the northern hemisphere for Christmas and see what the celebrations are like in the freezing cold."

"I don't think I'd like the idea of not being able to play backyard cricket after Christmas lunch."

"We won't be playing cricket tomorrow," Zac said, suddenly sobering. He looked into her eyes and then kissed her. "Better set that movie going before I get distracted."

They only got to the ghost of Christmas present before the movie was interrupted.

"Dad!" Maddie jumped up from the couch when she saw her father and Ellen enter the lounge room. Zac hadn't seen Jimmy since the Medal Count dinner. He'd talked to him on Skype a number of times, especially to ask permission to marry his daughter. But he suddenly remembered what a dynamic personality Jimmy Grace was when he walked into the house.

"You've managed to keep out of trouble, I see," Jimmy said to Zac as he shook his hand. "You better do the right thing by my daughter."

"Dad!" Maddie objected. "Don't be so intimidating. He's not one of your players anymore."

Zac held Jimmy's gaze, still trying to figure out if Jimmy was joking or saying something more serious and demanding.

"Cut it out," Maddie said. "Don't forget I'm still the one with the whistle."

Jimmy backed down and gave a grin. "You're not going to let her continue umpiring, are you?"

"Why not?" Zac asked. "She's one of the best. I'm not going to mess with that."

Zac thought Jimmy might say something else, but he changed tack.

"Well, I wish you both all the best."

"Thanks, Dad," Maddie said. "I'm glad you're here."

"I only have one daughter. I wasn't going to miss giving you away at your wedding."

"How long a break have you given your team over Christmas?" Zac asked.

"Nearly three weeks. Then it's back to work. You?"

"About the same."

Nina came into the room and greeted the newly arrived visitors.

"Come into the kitchen," she said. "I have some Christmas baking and cold fruit punch."

Zac flicked off the TV and caught Maddie's hand before she followed the rest of the family out. "I guess we probably should start to get ready soon. Are you okay with what we've arranged?"

"Of course. Why?"

"Just what Ali said this morning, you know, pink swans and all."

"I'm just as happy to get married in the sand with bare feet," Maddie said.

"I've only got an open neck shirt. No jacket and tie."

"The less clothes to get off, the better."

Zac pretended shock at her statement, but then laughed. "That is the last I can spend with you today. You're more trouble than I can manage."

"That's just as well. Ali's friend is due here shortly, and then the groom can't see the bride until tonight."

Chapter Ten

Maddie had bought a simply cut dress that came to just above her ankles. It was overlaid with lace, and had an elegant satin band around her waist.

"You look like a hipster," Ali said.

"Perfect," Maddie replied. "That's just the look I was going for."

"Are you sure about the shoes?"

"Ali, stop worrying. We're all wearing bare feet. We'll be on the sand some of the time, and shoes would be a nuisance."

Maddie fixed a fine silver chain around her ankle, then stood up and surveyed herself in the mirror.

"I hope those flowers in your hair don't wilt in this heat."

"Ali!" Maddie frowned at her.

Ali laughed. "Okay, I give up. You look beautiful, in a rustic sort of way."

"So you think Zac will like it?"

"Pfft! Zac? He wouldn't care if you were in a flour sack. That boy's completely lost his mind over you."

"Good." Maddie turned from the mirror and smiled at her soon-to-be sister. "You look pretty smart yourself, Ms Beecham."

"I'm not sold on the bare feet."

"You can wear heels if you like. Good luck with the sand."

The heat of the day merged into a balmy summer's night. Maddie could hear the carols being sung from the park down the road.

"When do you want to go to the park?" Jimmy asked.

"Just as soon as the sun's gone down. I want to sneak to the back of the crowd without being a spectacle."

"You'll be a spectacle, all right," Ali said. "As soon as that crowd realize what's going on, all eyes will be on you."

"That's why I don't want to get there until it's nearly dark."

The time came soon enough. The small wedding group walked the short distance to the park, guided by the dim street lights and glowing trees. They joined the back of the assembled crowd just in time to hear the minister give a Christmas address.

"As we join hearts with people all around the world, celebrating the coming of our Savior, why don't you join with the band as we sing our favorite carol, *Silent Night?*"

The band began to play the introduction, and children all around the park held up their colored glow sticks ready to wave them in the air in time to the music. It was a wonderful Christmas feel. Maddie shivered with excitement.

This Christmas Eve was going to be more exciting than any she'd ever experienced before.

The Carols by Candlelight Christmas festivities finished once the crowd had sung *Jingle Bells* and Santa had arrived on the back of a tray-top ute. Maddie smiled as she heard the MC give the usual excuse about why there was no reindeer or sled—it was too hot for snow in the Australian summer. Last time Maddie had been at a community carols event, Santa had arrived on a motorbike. She watched as the children swarmed to visit with the grand old gentleman, then searched the crowd until she spotted Zac with one of his footy mates.

"They look so cool, don't they?" Maddie whispered to Ali.

Ali shrugged. "He could have worn a tie."

"No way," Maddie said. "I love this casual look." She had suggested the white open-necked shirt with braces, and plain camel-colored trousers, rolled up at the bottom. As agreed, guys had bare feet too. This was going to be a summer beach wedding. Though the stage was set up on the grassy park area, it gave way to the beach on the southern side of the park. They could hear the waves lapping the shore.

"Uh oh! It looks like you're on," Ali whispered.

The children seemed happy now that they'd each been given their icy-pole and lolly bag from Santa. The minister was mounting the temporary stage and took the microphone in hand again.

"Just a quick announcement from Zac Beecham for family, friends, and interested locals. If you have the time, you're cordially invited to stay and witness Zac's marriage to his gorgeous fiancée, Maddie Grace."

There was an enthusiastic response from the crowd. Though many of them had already packed up to go home, most of them came back and spread their blankets back down, and unfolded their camp chairs. This was an invitation too good to miss.

Jimmy appeared from the shadows.

"Okay, Maddie. This is it. You sure this is what you want?"

"I would have told you long before now if it wasn't," she said. "Come on Dad. You love Zac. Admit it."

"I do like him, very much. I couldn't have chosen a better man for you."

"Great. Then let's get on with this, shall we."

Jimmy held out his arm, and the small wedding party waited until the music began to play over the sound system. The moment they started walking towards the front of the crowd, all eyes turned to watch them. Maddie felt her smile stretch wide. Zac's gaze had zeroed in on her almost straight away, and the look on his face was so captivating, Maddie thought she might faint from happiness before she even reached him.

By the time Jimmy had handed her to Zac, Maddie's heart was beating madly.

Zac leaned in close to her and whispered for her ears alone: "You're gorgeous, Maddie. I'm so glad I'm marrying you tonight."

"Care to share with the crowd?" The minister's good-humored question brought a lot of laughter from those observing.

The ceremony didn't take long, and then the minister gave Zac the opportunity to kiss his bride. The crowd broke into loud cheers and clapping. Maddie heard it, and eventually the pair of them had to smile at the response. Otherwise, they would have kept on kissing.

"All right. That's enough for now." The minister kept up with the banter. "Let's all pray for the happy couple now, and then we can send them on their way."

Still holding Zac's hand, Maddie bowed her head and listened while the minister prayed for wisdom, courage and blessing over their marriage.

"Amen."

Again the crowd broke into loud enthusiastic cheering.

Nina, Rod, Jimmy, and Ali all came forward and offered their love and congratulations with hugs and kisses. It happened way too fast, and then it was over.

"Okay, folks," the minister said. "That's the end of our Christmas festivities. Merry Christmas to you all."

Not many people moved. They were keen to watch the wedding party leave.

"Are you having a celebration supper tonight?" The minister asked after he'd dismissed the crowd.

"Not tonight," Zac answered. "We'll celebrate over Christmas lunch tomorrow afternoon."

"Where will you go tonight?" he asked.

Zac winked at him. "That's classified information. But thank you for your beautiful blessing. We really appreciate you taking the time on Christmas Eve."

"Are you kidding? My kids are totally thrilled that they got to see their favorite footy star get married, and that I got to marry him. Best Christmas present they've ever had."

Max arrived at that moment with the one photographer who had been given the exclusive right to take photos. They went through the motions of having some photos taken that one women's magazine would have as their cover for the next edition.

Maddie didn't mind too much. She was with Zac. For the most part, he had his arms around her, and spoke to her at every opportunity they got.

"Okay, that's enough for now," Max finally said. "Thank you for coming."

"Thanks for the opportunity," the photographer said.

"Now our happy couple need to leave."

"Thanks, Max," Zac said. "Where did you leave my car?"

"I'll drop you there."

Maddie took the last minute to kiss her dad, Ali and her new parents-in-law.

"Have a great night," Ali said, waggling her eyebrows at her.

Maddie smiled. "See you tomorrow, sis."

***

Zac held open the car door of his late model sports car. Maddie buckled the seat belt, and as soon as Zac got in the driver's side, she leaned across and kissed him.

"I love you," she said.

"I love you."

"So where are we going?"

Zac smiled. "Not far."

"Good. I'm tired of waiting for you."

This time he laughed. They drove a few moments in silence, before Zac spoke again.

"You haven't been with a guy before, have you?" he asked. "I'm sorry. I probably should have asked you that before now, but I assumed."

"No, I have not. Zachary Beecham. I've been waiting for you all my life. I thought you knew this."

"We didn't actually discuss your love life. It was only mine that everybody seemed to be obsessed with."

"Well, set your mind at ease. I've been too busy to be messing around with guys who don't mean anything to me."

"Me too—too busy waiting for you, I mean."

"So we are a strange pair in this day and age, aren't we?"

"How so?"

"Mid-twenties and neither of us have any sexual experience."

"I'm not sorry. I can't imagine having had other women and then trying to offer you the best of me."

"I know we're as old-fashioned as horse and cart, but I'm really glad—it's a first time for both of us."

Zac let go a deep sigh.

"What's that all about?"

"I've been doing some study on purity, and it's not just about being old-fashioned."

"What do you mean?"

"I've read some papers from 'experts' who believe it's a dangerous idea to teach young people abstinence. Like it's healthy for emotional development to just follow our sexual urges, and have recreational sex, so long as it's safe sex and consensual."

"I can't get my head around that."

"You really are old fashioned, aren't you?"

"Are you sorry?"

"Not at all. I still think it's worth waiting. I've married you for life, you know that?"

"That's what you said in our vows."

"Anyway, enough talking. We're here."

Maddie was surprised. They'd taken a winding route through various streets around the town, and arrived at a house that was only a short drive from his parents' house. He opened the garage with a remote control and parked the car inside, then closed the door.

"Whose house is this?" Maddie asked.

"Mine."

"Yours? Since when?"

"I've had it for a few years. I let it out as a holiday house."

"Is this one of your investments for your post-football years?"

"It is. I'd like to come back here and live when I finish playing, but I have to talk to my wife about that first. Just in case she wants to go and live in Perth."

Maddie laughed. "I don't care where I live, so long as I live with you."

Zac leaned across and kissed her again, but instead of it being a quick peck, they lingered and it grew passionate and heated. Zac twisted and tried to close the distance, but the gear console got in the way. Maddie broke the kiss and laughed.

"I assume this house of yours has a bedroom," she said.

"A couple," Zac replied.

"I think we only need one."

With that, Zac leaped out of the driver's door, and was around her side in a flash, opening her door, and helping her out. Maddie couldn't help laughing, she was so full of joy. He opened the door to the main house, and before she knew what was happening, he'd scooped her up in his arms. She threw her arms about his neck and continued with the kissing fest. He carried her into the house, kicked the door shut behind him, and took her to the first available bedroom.

***

Maddie couldn't help the smile that was on her face when she arrived at the Beecham's house for Christmas lunch. Her father and Ellen were there as well.

"You look happy," Jimmy said when they walked in.

"Of course they look happy," Ali said. "They just got married."

Maddie blushed. She didn't really want to talk with her father and in-laws about what she and Zac had shared.

"Well, we're here to celebrate our marriage and Christmas all at once, so I hope it's all ready, because I don't want to stay too long," Zac said.

Maddie saw the smirks and knowing looks the family shared. She didn't want to stay too long either. She'd just experienced her husband. She wanted to experience him again.

Nina and Ali had the meal organized, the traditional roast dinner with all the trimmings, just like every Christmas Maddie had ever had. The Christmas tree and decorations. Christmas bonbons and serviettes with a holly print. Christmas pudding with brandy custard.

Because it was a hot day, they had cooked the ham and turkey in the outdoor Weber barbeque, but they still cooked the roast vegetables inside. The air conditioners were blowing on high to keep the house at a bearable level.

"I'd like to propose a toast to our newly married couple," Rod said, after they finished the pudding. "I worried that Zac would get tangled up with too many girls when he first rose to fame, and then I worried that he wouldn't find any woman at all. So when he finally ran one over during a football game, Nina and I thought that perhaps God had answered our prayers and found one for him."

"Thanks, Dad," Zac mumbled. "It wasn't really the best way to meet a girl."

"It was effective, and got the job done. We're pleased as punch to have you as our new daughter, Maddie. We want to wish you both all the best."

"Thanks, Rod," Maddie said.

"Jimmy?" Rod turned towards their guest.

"I've had Maddie in and around young, virile athletes for years. They knew that Maddie was to be respected and there would have been serious consequences if any of them had crossed the line. I never had any trouble with her and the boys. But as years went by I began to worry that I'd made her immune to men. But I have to say, of all the players I've had charge of, Zac is the only one I would have been happy to have as a son-in-law. I'm sorry I didn't introduce you in a more conventional way, Zac. It was a little dramatic the way you did it."

"Thanks, Dad," Maddie said.

"But it was a stroke of genius by me asking Zac to look after Maddie in the hospital, don't you think?"

"It got us into a lot of trouble," Maddie said. Zac squeezed her hand.

"The Australian public have moved on," Jimmy replied.

"Not so much," Ali said. "Did you see the report in this morning's *Herald* online?"

"Oh, did they put a story about the wedding?" Nina asked.

"You could say that." Ali got up to get her tablet. She opened and scrolled to find the report. She took the tablet over for Jimmy to see. He laughed, and passed it around to Zac. Maddie peered over his shoulder at the headlines.

REV MARRIES THE REF

Then the by line: What now: First knocked out, then knocked up?

> Zac turned a worried look to Maddie.
> "Sounds like a plan," Maddie said.
> Zac smiled and winked at her.

WHERE THERE'S SMOKE

by MEREDITH RESCE

Where There's Smoke

Golden Grain Publishing

PO Box 880 Unley SA 5061

The National Library of Australia Cataloguing-in-Publication entry:

Creator: Resce, Meredith, 1963 – author.

Title: Where there's smoke / Meredith Resce.

ISBN: 9780977592760 (ebook)

Subjects: Forest fires--South Australia--fiction

Dewey Number: A823.3

Though 'Where There's Smoke' is inspired by an actual bushfire event from January 2014, it is a work of fiction. Names, characters and incidents are either the product of the author's imagination or are used fictitiously, and any resemblance to actual events or persons, living or dead, is entirely coincidental.

Available also as an eBook download

Contemporary Drama; Romance.

Cover Art by: IT Girl Designs - www.ItGirlDesigns.com

Photographs: Fire in Forest © SURZ

Side view of a couple standing on forest trail and hugging © nosnibor137

Author Note

This short story is inspired by a real bushfire event that occurred in January 2014. After a band of thunderstorms passed through South Australia, hundreds of fires were lit, some on open plain country, and some in inaccessible bushland. Right across the state, emergency services were stretched to the limit.

One of the worst fires was named 'The Bangor Fires' which eventually burned for a number of weeks. While a number of homes and properties were lost, thankfully there was no loss of human life. It is in times of crisis like this that one can witness the true spirit of community and togetherness.

Other than being inspired by this real event, this story is a complete work of fiction. The Miller and Noble family do not exist, except in my imagination.

17Th January 2014
South Australia

'I don't get why you had to come all this way.'

Chris ignored Sienna's comment. It was hot and the car air-conditioning was struggling to keep up. He was uncomfortable with the sticky sweat that had gathered on his hairline and was tempted to roll the window down just to let some air blow across his face, but he knew it would be hot wind and Sienna would then have something else to complain about.

'It's not like you live there anymore.' Sienna continued complaining, apparently oblivious to Chris's irritation and he clamped his teeth together to keep from snapping at her.

'What good do you think you can do?' she said. 'If your family can't look out for their own property I don't think your rushing up country is going to make any difference.'

'Look, Sienna, would you mind just being quiet please.' Chris was as polite as he could be. There were a lot of other words that he really wanted to say, but he wasn't the sort to speak harshly on a normal occasion.

'It's so bloody hot, Chris. Honestly, we could have gone to the beach today.'

'Do you mind?' It was past normal and Chris's patience had worn thin.

'I do, actually. I think we should have stayed in the city.'

'I think *you* should have stayed in the city. I didn't ask you to come.'

Sienna turned a malevolent look in his direction. Chris could feel her eyes boring into him and expected that she would either break into tears or sulk next. He chose not to say anything more. He didn't really want to think about his companion at the moment. The closer he got to home the more he could see and smell the smoke. A bushfire out of control heading toward his family home was making him feel sick with anxiety.

'You're a real bastard, you know that.'

'Sienna, please! I don't swear at you, I'd appreciate it if you would mind your language. I'm sorry you aren't happy, but I'm a little preoccupied at the moment.'

'I can see that! I can really see just how important I am to you.'

Chris rolled his eyes. He had no wish to even think about Sienna or what she thought about in terms of a relationship. He wished he'd had the guts to just tell her she wasn't welcome on this urgent trip, but he didn't. As usual, he'd hedged, hinted and hoped she'd get the message. She'd whined and cajoled and stubbornly refused to get his meaning. Finally he'd given in and she now sat in his car as they neared the end of the three and a half hour trip from the city to his childhood home.

'There's so much smoke.'

'It's a major bushfire. What do you expect?'

'There's no need to be testy.'

Chris swallowed another retort. The bickering was stupid and he really couldn't be bothered especially since they were now only a few minutes from their destination. As he rounded the bend he was now driving directly towards Mount Remarkable. Any tourist would think they were driving straight into the side of a solid mountain, but he knew the town was nestled right at the foot of the huge mountain. He'd seen all the smoke hanging over the ranges from Wirabarra heading north, and now was glad to see that the fire hadn't yet reached as far as Melrose. The argument with Sienna faded completely as his mind became engaged with what he was seeing as he drove within the town limits. He couldn't believe the hive of activity that was in the street around the CFS shed. Melrose was only ever busy a few times a year on major public holidays. Usually you'd be lucky to see more than four cars in the street at one time. Today there were official vehicles of every size and shape representing all of the emergency services: CFS, MFS, SES, and other acronyms that represented emergency personnel. Then there were farm four-wheel-drive vehicles lined up along the side of the road, each one with a fire-fighting unit loaded on the back. Chris looked closely to see if his father was anywhere amongst the crowd, but couldn't see him. He pulled over and got out of the car.

'Where are you going?' Sienna called after him.

'Be back in a minute,' he replied. He'd only taken two steps across the road when he was greeted.

'Hey, Chris!'

'Joe.' Chris returned the casual greeting of one of the farmers he knew who lived out on the plain away from the mountain and heavy bushland. 'What's the situation?'

'Not good, mate.' Joe shook his head. 'It's headed in your folk's direction. Right out of control. If you've a mind to go up into the hills and help evacuate, you'd better move now. Another hour or so and it'll be too dangerous.'

'Is that the official word?' Chris nodded toward the emergency headquarters that had been set up in the CFS sheds.

'You can check. The roads up that way are closed to traffic, but they might let a local in to defend property. Have you got a unit?'

'Nah! Just got in from Adelaide.'

'You can take my unit if you need. We've just come in from putting out one of the grass fires on the plain, but they only want CFS trained volunteers out in the hills at the minute. They'll probably let you go to help your folks defend the property though. But you'd better hurry.'

'Thanks, Joe.'

Chris knew which vehicle was Joe's and knew the keys would be in the ignition. Where else would they be. He hurried back across the road to his own car and opened the door.

'I'm taking a fire fighting unit up to our place. You'll have to go to the pub and wait there.'

'Can't I come with you?' Sienna whined.

'No! Are you crazy? It's a bushfire, not a picnic, Sienna. I haven't got time to argue with you about it.' He tossed his keys to her and turned back towards Joe's vehicle.

'Good luck, mate,' Joe said. 'I'll be thinking of you.'

Chris jumped into the borrowed farm vehicle and put it into gear. Taking the Survey road that led up into the hills behind the town was automatic for him. It was a dusty unsealed road, but it was the road home. But his heart hammered with anxiety as he saw the billows of black smoke south toward Murray Town. He could see which way the wind was blowing by the trees that were bending as if they were being pulled. Thankfully it wasn't in his direction. There were cops at the first cross roads out of the town, detouring traffic away. Chris pulled over.

'Road's closed. Oh, hi Chris.' It was Phil, the local cop from Booleroo Centre.

'Mum and Dad are still out there, I take it?' Chris asked.

'I haven't seen them come out yet. Not sure if they plan to evacuate or stay to defend the farm. Your sister-in-law hasn't brought the kids out yet though.'

'Tim and Sue are in Phuket. First time they take a big family holiday and their farm comes under fire.'

'So your folks are out there on their own?'

'They were house-sitting and taking care of the animals while Tim and Sue were away. Can you let me through? I'll need to help them get stock out if we still can.'

'Just let me check to see where the fire front is and how fast it's moving.'

Phil took a few moments on his radio to get the information before coming back.

'Better move it, Chris. It's not travelling too fast at the moment, but you can't tell with these winds.'

Chris drove around the road block sign and put his foot down. The smoke haze wasn't too bad and he guessed the wind wasn't exactly blowing in their direction at the moment, but he knew that later in the day there would be a wind change and it would swing around and blow a gully wind in their direction. There wasn't time to be sitting around thinking what to do.

***

'As soon as we get to town and unhook the horse float, I'll come straight back,' Ken Noble said to his daughter. Sally watched as her father climbed up into the old truck. They'd put hurdles on the back and had loaded the four milking cows and about twenty sheep. There was a grinding of gears and the old girl gave a tired groan as it moved slowly into action.

'Are you sure you should stay?' Wendy Noble asked.

'We have to try to defend the farm, Mum,' Sally replied. 'I'll get busy filling the gutters and hosing the house down. Just get those horses out of the hills and down on the plain away from the fires.'

'I'd feel better if you'd come with me.'

'I can't, Mum. This is my place now. I've got to try to defend it.'

Wendy gave a nod and got into their SUV. Sally watched her mother give a sad wave and then put her vehicle into gear and begin to follow the truck, towing the horse-float behind.

I'd feel better if someone was here with me.

Noble Park was her place now. Sally's mother and father had recently bought a place for their retirement in the town and had begun to transfer their gear down a few weeks ago, though they hadn't quite finished the move yet. But as soon as they'd received the emergency evacuation warning text, they'd all begun to pack irreplaceable items into suitcases and plastic tubs. There was simply no time to do a proper pack anymore. And the animals were irreplaceable to Sally. She'd recently bought some ewes and two stud rams to trial a new breed of sheep. They'd loaded the rams and some of the ewes on the truck, but hadn't been able to fit them all. There were still another thirty or so locked in the stock yards. Sally worried about them. It wasn't just the strong acrid smell of eucalyptus burning in the air; she could see the billowing clouds of smoke off to the south. The predictable wind change would bring the danger right in their direction and Sally didn't know if she would be able to protect the remaining animals.

Pulling out her mobile phone she dialled her brother-in-law's number.

'Hi, this is Justin. Can't get to the phone at the moment. Leave a message.'

'Where are you, Justin?' she muttered.

Sally scrolled through to her other brother-in-law.

'Hey, Sal!' Brenton answered straight away.

'You can't get your fire unit up here to help defend my place I suppose.'

'Where's your dad?' Brenton asked.

'He and mum have just left with some of the stock. Can you come?'

'Sorry, Sal. We've got a situation out near us as well. That bloody dry lightening has lit fires all over the plain.'

Sally had all but forgotten the thunderstorm that had passed through the district several hours before. The air had been thick with humidity, but no moisture had fallen. Only hundreds of lightning strikes, and in these dry summer conditions, that meant fires. Living in the hills, Sally had forgotten about the farmers out on the plain. Fighting blazes in the open country was a relatively simple job, unlike what they would face in the thick and hilly bushland. Brenton's report brought her thoughts back to her sister.

'Are Bec and the kids safe?'

'Yeah. Bec loaded everything up and has headed over to Port Augusta to my mother's.'

'Do you know where Justin is?'

'He's out here with me. Sorry Sal. We really gotta get this grass fire under control. I know it's worse up in the hills, but...'

'Don't worry about it. I suppose Justin got Jen to safety.'

'Hold on, I'll ask him?'

Sally heard muffled conversation for a few moments before Justin's voice came on the line.

'Sal, I sent Jen to the hospital, to be honest. She's so near her due date I thought it would be best if she was in the right place in case something else happened.'

'Right.'

'Gotta go, Sal. Sorry.'

'Right.'

So this was what it was like to be a single farmer. At least she didn't have kids and a spouse to worry about like her sisters. Sally slipped the phone in her pocket. She was on her own for at least an hour. Her dad wouldn't be able to get to town in that old truck and get back before then.

There was nothing to do but take action. She got the ladder from the shed, and some old rags and plastic bags. She'd been up on the roof for about fifteen minutes, clearing as much dry leaves and twigs out of the gutter as possible, and shoving the plastic covered rags into the downpipes. She kept looking up at intervals to see what the smoke was doing, trying to gauge if it was getting any closer, when she saw something that nearly made her heart stop.

'Chris Miller. You sure picked a fine time to return home.'

Sally could see the Miller's yard from the roof. Their houses were only a matter of two or three hundred metres apart. Chris Miller. Now there was a long unresolved history. Fire or no fire, she wondered how he was. She couldn't help it.

'After these gutters are full, I think I'll see if you need a hand.'

***

'I'll just get these animals to safety, then I'll come back and help you.' Rob Miller slid the bolt securing the gate on the hurdles. There were about sixty or so sheep squashed into the back of his truck.

'What about your foot?' Chris cast a doubtful look at his father's moonboot. 'I can't believe you didn't tell me you'd broken your leg.'

'What's to tell? You're just like your mother, fussing too much.'

Chris shrugged his shoulders. He'd arrived at the farm earlier to find his father riding the quad bike having spent the morning mustering sheep from out in their hilly pastures. His mother was upset that her husband had been out alone and injured.

'Stop fussing,' Rob had snapped. 'We have to get this stock out, and there wasn't time to wait for Chris.'

Chris had felt a wave of guilt. Why did he live in the city? Why wasn't he here on the farm like a normal farmer's son? It was the change of wind that made them stop arguing and realise the danger was now definitely heading in their direction. Chris was thankful he was there to help yard the animals and drive them up the loading ramp onto the back of the truck.

'What are you going to do?' Chris's mother, Karen came over to them just as they'd got the truck secure. 'I've got the car loaded and ready to go. Are you coming with us?' She directed the question to her son.

'No!' Rob answered. 'He's going to stay and get ready to defend the place.'

'On your own?' Karen was ready to re-start the argument.

'No, I'll come back as soon as these animals are safe,' Rob said.

'No you won't! You're injured. You can hardly walk!'

'Well what do you expect me to do? Just leave the place to burn?'

'Look, we haven't got time to sort this out now,' Chris intervened. 'Just get these animals out of here. I'll do what I can to get the place defended.'

'I think you should come with us,' Karen said.

Rob shot her a look that said he was losing patience.

'I'm going to stay, Mum. We've still got a heap of sheep yarded and I need to do my best to defend them. They say a well prepared place has a good chance of survival.'

'Clear and fill the gutters, hose the walls, make sure the house is completely shut up, and turn on the watering system.' Rob listed things unnecessarily. Chris had already got these things on his to-do list.

'I reckon the fire will come down on us from the south-west, so have the fire-units set up on that side.'

'Is Tim's unit full and ready to use?' Chris asked. When he'd arrived at the farm he'd realised that Joe's unit was nearly empty and he'd already put the hose in to begin to refill it.

'It's ready.'

'I'm leaving now,' Karen said. 'I hope we're not too late.'

'You'll have to drive the truck,' Rob said. 'I can't manage the clutch with this foot.'

'I realise that.' Her stress was showing in her tone. 'We better get going.'

Chris kissed his mother and shook his dad's hand. They all knew they wouldn't make it back to help him defend. It was going to be up to him. He watched his Dad drive the automatic sedan they'd bought for their retirement, following the large truck full of stock. His mum looked out of place as driver of such a large vehicle. He knew she'd driven it many times in her younger years, but once her sons had grown up there hadn't been any need for her to be the extra driver. Today was different. With his brother on holiday somewhere in South-East-Asia, and his dad injured, Karen Miller's ability to drive the truck was a God-send. He shot up a prayer that they would get out of the hills before the fire bore down on them and closed the roads.

***

Sally drove her 4WD with fire unit down the tree lined drive they shared with the Millers. She was in a turmoil of ambiguity. She wanted to see Chris and she didn't want to see him. He'd disappeared from her life three years ago without a word, and hadn't spoken to her since. For a couple of friends who had been inseparable since kindergarten she didn't get it, and she realised it had hurt her a great deal. Added to these uncertain feelings was the anxiety of knowing there was a major bushfire bearing down upon them and she was on her own – except for him. She'd watched Karen and Rob Miller drive away and guessed they were doing exactly what her parents were doing—evacuating.

She drove around the Miller house and found Chris on the tractor on the south-western side. With the grader blade attached to the front of the tractor, he was moving a heap of fallen branches further away from the house. He didn't see her at first until she was standing on the ground basically in his path. That first eye contact yielded a huge smile, which made her stomach flip, but he obviously clamped down that emotion and an expression she couldn't read replaced the smile. He pulled the tractor up and jumped out of the cab.

'Hey, Sal! You got trouble?'

'Not yet,' she replied. 'But won't be long by the look of that smoke.'

'I saw your folks drive past a while ago. You got anybody else here to help defend your place?'

Sally shook her head. 'Brenton and Justin have a grass fire out on the plain. Dad reckons he's coming back, but I doubt he'll make it.'

'Do you need me to help get your place ready?'

Again she shook her head. 'I've done all I can until the flames get here. Can I help you?'

'Please.' Now Sally could read his facial expression. He was worried. 'Dad broke his leg and hasn't been able to get the gutters cleared.'

'I heard about his leg,' Sally said. 'Where's your ladder. I'll get on with it.'

'I think Tim has it stored in the car shed.'

Sally didn't stay to continue any discussion, but headed toward the car shed to get on with the job of preparing the Miller's gutters. If it hadn't been for the acrid smell of smoke and the strong wind blowing it in their direction she would have insisted Chris sit down and tell her exactly what he'd meant by just clearing off with no warning. Even as she walked around the back of the house, she was surprised to feel an anger that surged when she thought about Chris and the silence that had existed between them since he left those years ago. It was only the imminent danger that kept her on course. Now was obviously not the time to examine deep feelings. She was glad that at least she wasn't on her own in this fight to protect the property. She knew they'd work together like they always had in the past.

***

Chris had graded a good piece of ground around the sheep yards. Luckily there weren't many trees around that area. After he'd put the tractor back in the shed he'd pulled both Joe's and Tim's fire units around the south-western side of the house ready to fight. He knew it wouldn't be too much longer. The wind was gusting he estimated in excess of seventy kilometres per hour and a fire under such conditions would be travelling at least that fast. He turned on the watering system, and used an extra garden hose to water down the walls of the house. By the time he'd finished all this, Sally descended the ladder. Chris clamped his thoughts tight. He knew he wanted to think about Sally, but not now.

'We need to put that hose up in the gutters,' she said, holding her hand out to take it from him. He passed it over without comment.

'Can you find a rock or brick to hold it in place while it fills?'

Chris picked up one of the border rocks his sister-in-law, Sue, had around the flowerbeds.

'We better get inside and get some proper protective gear on, Sal,' Chris said as he handed her the rock.

There was too much anxious tension for there to be much conversation, and Chris was glad that despite three years of absence, he and Sally understood each other. They went around to the back of the house and into the back porch.

110

'Where does Tim keep his fire fighting gear?' Sally asked.

'I really don't know. You check the cupboards out here and I'll check in their bedroom.' As he walked down the hallway towards his brother's bedroom, Chris pulled his phone from his pocket. Scrolling through, he found his mum's mobile number and pressed call.

'Hi Mum,' he said when he heard her answer. 'Did you make it down to the town OK?'

'Only just,' she replied. 'I'm sorry I was so snappy. I'm really worried about you.'

'Listen, Mum, sorry to throw this at you, but can you go to the pub and find Sienna. I left her in town when I came out here.'

'Which pub?'

'Not sure. Probably the North Star.'

'Not the smartest time to bring your girlfriend to meet us,' Karen said.

'Not my girlfriend. Didn't bring her to meet you.'

'Why's she here, then?'

'No time to explain now. Can you contact the CFS and see if they have any units nearby. We're going to need them.'

'I'll let you know,' she replied. 'What do you want me to do with Sienna?'

'I don't know, Mum. Use your imagination.'

'Now who's being snappy? She is your girlfriend.'

'Mum...'

'All right. I'll call the CFS and let you know.'

Chris had been unable to find Tim's fire fighting protective gear in his rummage through their wardrobe and had turned to go back to the porch. He was still talking to his mother when he ran into Sally. She held up the Hi-Viz overalls, plastic goggles and a white protective hat she must have found in the porch cupboard.

'It's here, Chris.'

He nodded to her as he finished talking to his mother.

'What about you?' He looked concerned as he put his mobile phone away in his pocket. 'Have you got any protective gear at your house?'

She shrugged her shoulders. 'I was considering joining the CFS just for the gear, but I hadn't got around to it yet.' She gave a weak grin.

'Well that stuff you're wearing isn't any good for fighting a fire.' He looked at her cut-off denim shorts and t-shirt. The best she had on was her riding boots. 'You better go home and get something that will cover you better.'

'Do you think I should stay there or would it be more effective if we teamed up and fought this thing together.'

Chris thought for a minute. He wanted her to stay—foremost because he didn't want to face this alone, but also because they would be more effective fighting together. But then her place would be completely undefended until the pair of them could leave Tim's and move. He guessed the fire would move faster than that.

'I don't know, Sal. I can't make that decision.'

'Help me out, Chris.' She sounded stressed. 'I don't know what the best thing to do is.'

'Let's go out and see how much time we have.'

But when they stepped outside the smoke was thick and they could hear the roar of flames in the scrub to the south-west. There wasn't time to decide.

∗∗∗

'Here.' Chris threw the overalls, goggles and hat at her.

Sally's fingers fumbled with the press buttons on the overalls as she tried to fasten them. The legs were too long but she couldn't seem to get the bottoms rolled up properly as her hands shook. The sound of the fire was there. She needed to be holding a hose. She needed the pump on her fire unit to be on. She hurriedly pulled the goggles over her eyes, thankful that they would help her see against the stinging smoke. Chris had rummaged in the porch cupboard further and found Tim's heavy protective jacket and another pair of goggles in the pocket. They both pulled protective masks over their nose and mouth. It was game time. Just as they emerged into the smoky outdoors Chris's phone rang. He looked at the call ID and swore.

'Your mum?' Sally asked.

'No! That women is so clueless.'

'Which woman?'

'Ah, a friend of mine from the city.' Chris sounded irked. 'She should have just stayed there. Now's not the time.'

Sally watched as Chris ran over to his brother's unit, set about thirty metres from the house, and set the pump going. Before long he had the hose ready. Sally couldn't help wondering about *that woman* for a few moments, but the emergency very quickly purged those thoughts from her mind. As far as she was concerned, this was the moment she was about to prove that a woman could be a landowner. She didn't have a husband or a brother, and her father and brothers-in-law weren't here. It was time to see if she had what it took to really fight.

She went back to her 4WD, got in and drove it around closer to the drive on the south-east side. Her hands shook as she tried to get the pump started on her unit.

'Grow up, Sal,' she said fiercely to herself. She knew how to start a fire pump. It had never been a problem before. The sweat that broke out on her brow was more than the stifling summer heat. Her anxious tension was at an all time high, and it was time to use all that adrenaline in facing this destructive monster as it bore down on them.

***

Chris placed himself on some open ground facing the oncoming flames. He wanted to keep them from coming closer to the house if he could. The greatest threat was the embers that were being blown in his direction, starting spot fires ahead of the front. They'd done all they could to protect the house, knowing that any embers landing in the gutters would now drown instead of finding dry leaves and twigs to kindle. But it was the huge old gum trees nearby that they couldn't protect. He didn't really have time to think as he responded by instinct to spot fires that started, hosing them down and putting them out as quickly as they began. He couldn't think about the main front that was bearing down on them. He hoped that the ground that had already burned and the damp ground might put a stop to it. Or at least the flames would burn around the house and not through it.

Then suddenly his attention was caught by the explosion to his left. Heart hammering fiercely he turned to see the first of the trees on the drive had burst into furious flames. He saw Sally there doing her best to defend from that side, but she couldn't do anything to stop the trees from burning. She could only try to prevent the flames from progressing closer to the house. Chris's stomached tightened with worry. Sally was his childhood sweetheart. At least that was how he'd seen it. Apparently that was not quite her perception of it. Still, to see her in such a dangerous position now did nothing to calm him. But he couldn't leave his own position. The fire was on them and the pair of them had to try to get it to burn around the house, and he hoped the sheds behind. He had his UHF radio tuned to the official CFS channel and was keeping an ear on the talk going between the fire headquarters and the units on the ground. He knew they were aware that he and Sally were there, that they were alone and that the fire was on them, but they couldn't get their units in. They were fighting on other fronts. There was talk of a water bomber helicopter coming in, but it was way too late for that.

✳✳✳

Sally couldn't do anything about the trees. The wind had the flames bursting from one tree to the next and it was like a fire tunnel all the way down the drive toward her house. She couldn't even drive down there to get into position and meet the fire head on as it threatened her property. She knew it was hopeless. But she wasn't prepared to collapse in despair just yet. She saw the Miller's sheep yards and saw the sheep moving about restlessly, obviously terrified by the smoke and the noise. She got into her vehicle and drove back towards the yards and positioned herself with her hose in hand warding the flames off from attacking the animals. So far she was successful in keeping the fire from spreading to the Miller's stock yards. As she persisted in hosing down lit grass and bush her jaw was clamped tight. She had shut her mind to what she knew: her own stock yards were undefended. She still had animals on her property that had no one there to save them. There was nothing she could do but fight for Tim's sheep, tears streaming down her face as she imagined she could hear the distressed bleating of her own animals.

✳✳✳

The dragon had passed by. Tim and Sue's house stood unscathed though they'd lost the tractor shed and hay shed. The sheep in the stock yard stood still, almost as if they were dazed by the brush with death. Chris knew that the scene further down the gully was vastly different. He didn't want to look too closely at it yet. He needed to get the fires in the trees properly doused before he could even think about what to do next. A glance across at Sally as she held her hose on the smoking remnant of a tree told him she was on auto pilot. His heart broke for her. He'd heard the cries of her sheep and had been as helpless to save them as she had been. He hadn't watched too closely, but he knew her house and sheds were on fire. There hadn't been anything either of them could do to prevent it. The wave of guilt came washing over him again. He should have been with her to protect her property. His father and brother should have been here to watch their home, and he should have helped Sally. It might have been the sting of smoke that caused his eyes to water and nose to run—but he knew it wasn't.

***

It had been an hour since the main fierce front had passed by consuming some of the Miller property and all of the Noble's buildings and yards. Chris hadn't spoken to Sally and she hadn't been able to form words to speak to him. They'd both done what they had to do to make sure that what they'd managed to save would stay safe—that no flare-ups would double back and make another attempt to destroy the rescued property. Sally had heard the CFS communications channel. Chris had called in and given a report. No one was going to come now as the fire had moved on to new vulnerable targets and the fire fighting teams had moved along with it. She didn't know if her parents would be able to get back or not. From the reports it sounded as if the main road leading from the town out through the hills to their place was still ablaze in many places. She knew she was going to have to call her parents to let them know she was OK. They would no doubt be worried sick. But she didn't know how she could speak. Eventually they made the call to her. She answered but when she tried to speak the words just stuck in her throat.

'Sal?' Ken Noble's voice sounded uncertain, almost fearful. 'Sal, are you all right?'

Up til this moment there had only been tears tracing down her face. Now there were waves of emotion that came out as choking sobs.

'Sal?' Ken persisted. 'Talk to me.'

Sally shook her head and turned to see that Chris was standing a few metres away from her. She held out the phone to him hoping he would be able to do what she could not.

***

Chris stepped over and took the phone from her. 'Ken, it's Chris.'

'Are you all right up there?' Ken asked.

'I'm sorry, mate. Your place is gone.'

There was a heavy silence for a few moments.

'Is Sal all right?'

Chris was annoyed with himself. He should have reassured him on that count first. 'She's safe.'

'And you?'

'We're both safe. We managed to save Tim and Sue's house and sheep. They've lost a couple of sheds. I'm really sorry Ken.'

'We can't get out there,' Ken replied. 'The roads are closed. Too dangerous at the moment. Can you look after Sally?'

'We'll look after each other until you can get here,' Chris replied.

He closed Sally's phone and looked up to give it back to her. She was a mess. She'd flipped off the helmet some time ago and her hair was all over the place, despite the best efforts of the elastic hair band. Her face was streaked with soot and tears, and even now he could see she was really struggling.

'I'm sorry, Sal.' There wasn't anything else he could say. Instead he moved closer and they came together in an embrace that shared their grief and relief all at once.

***

117

The day had slipped away and darkness had descended and Sally hadn't noticed. Earlier Chris had gone with her to investigate her own losses. He'd held her hand when they came to the stock yards. Waves of emotion had flooded over her as she saw her animals burned, black and bloated, lying on the ground. She had wanted to be sick and to curl into a foetal position all at once, but Chris had held her upright. He'd been crying too. She could tell by the way his chest had shaken against her face. Words had been absolutely useless. By the time they'd got back to the Miller house she was emotionally and physically exhausted. She had nothing left.

'Why don't you take a shower?' Chris suggested. 'I'm going to keep an eye on the trees around the place to make sure there isn't any danger of smouldering wood that might flare up.' Sally knew the wind had died down, but that didn't mean a sudden gust might not cause things to go bad very quickly.

Sally just nodded and headed towards the bathroom. She was as familiar with this house as her own. She'd spent hours over here when she and Chris were kids. She noticed that Sue Miller had made some changes to decor since she'd taken over the house from Chris's mum. It was modern and nice. But then Sally thought of her own home, now a blackened mess of twisted metal and brick, and she started to convulse with sobbing again. This time Chris was outside and not there as a pillar of support. Instead she got under the cool stream of water and just let it run down her body. Fifteen minutes ticked past without her so much as reaching for a shampoo bottle. Eventually a banging on the bathroom door snapped her back into reality.

'Sal, are you all right?'

'I won't be long.' It had taken her an enormous amount of energy to shout the answer back, but she made the effort because she didn't want Chris breaking the bathroom lock to come in search of her. They had been the best of friends, but that was going too far. It only took a few minutes to shampoo and rinse her hair. She did notice that the cold shower was refreshing against the oppressive heat, but that was all she could feel. Everything else was numb. Then she looked at her shorts and t-shirt in a sooty dirty pile on the bathroom floor and she realised she didn't have a thing in the world to change into. She felt a wave of grief rise up again and she indulged it for a few moments, until she realised she couldn't just stand there naked forever. She grabbed one of the large bath towels and wrapped it around herself, then carefully unlocked the door.

'You OK?'

She had been hoping that Chris would still be outside, but he was sitting nearby as if he was anxious she might have gone down the drain hole.

'I'll need to borrow some clothes,' she said.

Suddenly Chris looked away. She had caught the glimpse of desire in his eyes, and it rocked her. This was stupid. They'd swum together a thousand times and not been coy when they'd got changed from their swimming gear. What was this sudden awareness of each other?

'I'll let you sort that out,' he said. 'I'll do another tree check. I'll take a shower after.' He was gone fairly quickly which was probably just as well.

Sally felt awkward going through Sue Miller's wardrobe and drawers, but what choice did she have. Sue was shorter than Sally and probably a size smaller so it hadn't been easy finding something to borrow. In the finish she'd opted to wear one of Tim's button down shirts, several sizes too large, and baggy enough to cover the other ill-fitting clothes she'd selected.

'I'm sorry, Sal.' Chris said it again the moment she walked back into the family room.

She just shrugged her shoulders. She didn't have any more tears at the moment.

'Did you pack a bag to send out with your parents?'

'Mum might have, I don't know. I was too busy helping Dad round up and load stock.'

'She would have taken something,' Chris said.

'Why don't you have a shower now?' Sally wanted to change the subject. 'I'll go and check the trees.'

'They're all right for the moment. I just checked them, and it's surprisingly still.'

'All the same.'

Chris shrugged and moved off towards the bathroom.

***

Chris had the same issue when he emerged from the bathroom, but he didn't think too much about dashing from the bathroom to his brother's bedroom wearing only a towel. He couldn't get Sally out of his head, and he was angry with himself about it. It had been over between them for three years and yet all he wanted to do was take her in his arms and never let her go.

Finally dressed in clean clothes with his longish hair still damp and straggly he stepped back into the family room.

'You want to eat something?' he asked.

'It's too late to eat,' Sally said.

Chris glanced across at the clock and saw it was nearing 11pm. He didn't argue. Swallowing food seemed like something too hard to think about at the moment.

'You want to sleep?'

'Do you think you could sleep after a day like today?' she asked.

'You want to talk?'

Sally paused for a moment and he could see something was turning over in her mind. Then she rounded on him with anger in her eyes.

'Well since you've brought it up, yes, I do want to talk.'

Chris came right into the room and chose a chair opposite the couch she was sitting on. Quite suddenly he felt he was about to be grilled.

'What made you disappear so suddenly like that?'

He knew she was talking about his decision three years earlier to take a job with the Agricultural Department in the city.

'I couldn't be here anymore Sal,' he said. 'Not after we broke up.'

Sally frowned at him.

'Well you might not have felt anything, but it destroyed me inside. I just couldn't face seeing you all the time.'

She continued to frown. He decided to stare her down. He felt it was a fair explanation.

'How could we have broken up?' Eventually she asked the question, but Chris was confused.

'It was fairly easy, apparently. For you, anyway.'

'No, I mean, how can we have broken something that never existed.'

'Oh, fine! Is that how you want to play it? All those years of being together, and you think we never existed.' He got up from his seat and prowled around agitated.

'Calm down,' she said. 'What we had for all those years—since we were kids—was friendship. My best friend, I would have said.'

'Yeah, so when you ended it, I couldn't stay.'

'I never ended our friendship.'

Chris was silent and felt almost sullen. He wanted to withdraw from the conversation. He'd never been great at communicating what he felt.

'But you knew I wanted more than friendship.'

'Did I? How was I supposed to know that?'

Chris was stumped. He'd never put that idea into words before. He just assumed that Sally had wanted what he'd wanted. Something closer.

'Well, what about that last night—at the footy breakup?'

'What about it?'

'You slapped me and told me to get lost.'

'You were drunk and tried to kiss me.'

'I thought you loved me.'

'I do love you, Chris Miller. I've always loved you. But I'm not just going to go all mushy when my best friend drinks himself stupid and then tries it on with me.'

Chris paused to think about all the things she'd said.

'Was I that drunk?'

'You were acting like a prize idiot, and I'd never seen you like that before.'

'I don't usually drink that much.'

'I know. That's what I couldn't understand.'

'I just wanted to get some courage to…you know…'

'Do I know, Chris? What are you trying to say?'

Chris was struggling. He was also a little annoyed. She knew what he meant, he was sure of it.

'I'm not great with speeches,' he said.

'I know that,' she answered.

He was searching deep within to find the right thing to say when his phone rang. It was Sienna. He didn't want to talk to her, but then he didn't know what he should say to Sally either.

'Here, can you answer this.' He threw the phone to Sally and walked out of the room to go outside to check on the trees yet again.

>**

Sally had been playing hardball. She had guessed Chris's feelings, and she probably returned them, but that night at the footy club, he'd turned into an octopus. His hands were everywhere and he was acting so badly she had slapped him. Really hard. She'd meant it too. She hadn't thought for a minute that he would then disappear for three years. She thought he would go home, wake up with a hangover and take a good hard look at his stupid decision. Then she had planned to talk to him. But she'd never got the chance. He had driven back to Adelaide for his last few weeks of uni, and he hadn't returned. Not to see her, anyway. Now, three years later, he'd just sat there and told her he had been heartbroken. Well he didn't know the half of it. So it took a major natural disaster to force them to face each other and she had hopes they could get it sorted this time. But she wasn't going to make it easy. Then his stupid phone had rung and he threw it to her to answer.

Who on earth is Sienna? She thought as she pressed answer. *That woman, I suppose.*

'Hi, this is Chris's phone.' She tried to sound cheery. It was nearly midnight, they'd had a hell of a day under huge stress and were on the verge of breaking down a stupid barrier. Why on earth she thought she needed to sound cheery she couldn't figure, but it was out now.

'Where's Chris?' A snappy female voice on the other end of the line chased the cheer away fairly quickly.

'He's outside checking the trees,' Sally answered. She could do snappy.

'I want to talk to him.'

'I'm sorry, he's not here at the moment.'

'Who are you, anyway?' Sienna asked.

'I'm Sally Noble. Chris's friend.'

'Yeah, well I'm Chris's girlfriend, so I hope you don't get any fancy ideas.'

Sally rolled her eyes. *Where did he pick this one up?* She mentally ran through several sharp replies, but decided it probably wasn't helpful to engage in a cat fight.

'Can you get him to call me back as soon as he gets inside?' Sienna said, then quickly disconnected the call.

'I might,' Sally muttered to herself. 'Or I might not.'

She flopped on the couch. That little attack had just used up the very last ounce of emotional energy she possessed. Suddenly she felt overwhelmed with tiredness. She leaned her head back against the couch and closed her eyes. A heavy cloud of fog was descending and she was happy to succumb to it.

***

Chris returned inside about half an hour later. He'd found a stump that had some glowing about it, so he'd taken an axe to it and then made sure it was properly extinguished. He was ready to continue the discussion with Sally. He'd thought about what he probably should say and as he had been swinging the axe he had engaged in some serious self-talk. *Stop being such a coward. She's your best friend. Tell her straight.*

But once he came into the family room he saw that she was dead to the world. His courage fled and he decided it was time he tried to sleep a bit too. There were plenty of beds in the house, but Chris didn't want to settle too soundly for the night. He wanted to keep somewhat alert to possible flare-ups. With this in mind he flicked off the light switch, then sat next to Sally on the couch. She responded in her sleep by snuggling up to him and laying her head on his shoulder. That wasn't very comfortable, so he put his arm around her and adjusted their position until he was comfortable.

I'll only sleep for a half hour, he told himself. But once his eyes were closed, he was gone for the night.

***

Sally sat bolt upright, her heart hammering away and her mind struggling to focus on where she was. Then her thoughts began to clear and she realised that she'd woken to the sound of people entering the house. As Chris's mum and dad walked into the room, followed by a very beautiful and stylish young woman, she also realised that Chris had sat up with her. They were still somewhat entangled in each other.

That must be Sienna, she thought as she saw the ugly scowl on her face. *Too late now!*

'Are you two all right?' Karen asked.

Sally wanted to leap to her feet and pretend they had been just sitting quietly for a moment, but her head was full of bricks and any movement this morning was going to have to be slow.

'What time is it?' Chris's voice came from just near her shoulder. He wasn't moving very quickly either, and he sounded half-asleep.

'It's past seven.' Amusingly, Rob almost sounded as if he were scolding them for still being asleep at this hour.

'So the road's open then?' Chris asked.

'Obviously,' Sally said.

'Actually it is still closed officially,' Rob answered his son, 'but they let us through being locals. I saw your mum, Sal, and they will be here in about fifteen minutes as well.'

Sally made a huge effort and managed to get herself upright on two legs. She still felt fairly wonky though. Yesterday had really taken a toll.

'I'll just go down to our place and wait for them,' she said.

She began to walk out of the Miller's family room when Chris followed quickly behind her. She continued outside.

'Hey, Sal. Can we finish our discussion from last night?'

'Not now, Chris.'

'Why?' He looked crestfallen.

'Because you have a girlfriend.'

'I don't have a girlfriend,' he defended.

Sally shook her head as if he were a hopeless case.

'Look, Chris,' she began, 'I don't know what you've said to her, or haven't said to her, but she thinks she is your girlfriend. I know you and just how good you are at communicating your feelings. You need to sort it out. You can't just ignore her because she believes something you didn't mean.'

'But what about us?'

'Now's not the time in any case.' She turned and began to walk away, but he took two long strides, reached out for her arm and pulled her to a stop.

'When, then?'

'You sort it out with Sienna, Chris, and I don't mean just dump it on her. The poor girl is probably really hurting after what she's seen this morning as it is. You need to talk to her properly.'

She removed Chris's hand and continued walking.

***

Chris watched Sally walk away and for a moment he felt like he should run after her and beg her forgiveness or pour out his heart or something dramatic. None of which were natural for him. But when he saw Wendy and Ken Noble's SUV come along the charred drive he knew she was right. Now was not the time. He watched a few more moments as Wendy got out of the passenger seat and mother and daughter caught

126

each other in an emotional embrace. They'd just lost their family home and farm. He wished he could have been a part of this exchange, but he knew he had his own emotional issues he must face, and it wasn't going to be easy.

***

Karen eventually came up with a solution to the dilemma. Even as she made the suggestion it sounded more like a decree. Chris knew she was upset with him.

'I'll come and pick you up from our place in about two hours', she said. 'That should give you enough time to sort this mess out.'

By mess Chris knew she was referring to the sullen, apparently hard-done-by Sienna who was even now sitting in the front of Joe's 4WD.

'How am I going to get back to Adelaide then?' he asked.

'Just go and sort your relationship dramas out,' Karen said.

'And make it quick, if you think that's possible,' Rob added. 'We've got a lot of clean up to do.'

Chris left his brother's house in an emotional turmoil. They still had smouldering gum trees to keep an eye on, they had stock they were going to have to try to find feed for and then he guessed they would assess the damage. But for now he had other damage that needed attention. Sienna had him by the scruff of the neck, so to speak, and he was going to have to regain control of his own life. He still wasn't sure how she'd come to the conclusion that they were an item—but then he admitted he wasn't being honest. Sally was right. He had noticed Sienna's possessive language and the way she was always manipulating situations so they were together. He'd thought she was probably taking too much for granted, but he had not had the courage to even try to broach the subject. Live and let live had been his motto - anything to

127

get out of confronting awkward situations. Now it was awkward with a capital A.

'Listen, Sienna.' He decided to come straight to the point even while they were driving back to his parent's house in the town. 'I'm really sorry you've misunderstood…'

'How could I misunderstand? You were sleeping with her on the couch.'

Chris blew out a breath of frustration. Highly charged emotional conversations were not his forte. He usually ran from them. Evidence—Sally.

'I mean you misunderstood what there was between you and me.'

Sienna glared at him, and though he kept his eyes on the road, he could feel it.

'I felt embarrassed telling you there was never going to be anything.'

'Oh, you're breaking my heart.'

'Well, if I'd told you to back off, you might have told me to get over myself thinking you were coming on to me.'

Sienna clamped her jaw shut and turned her eyes straight ahead. Chris only had to take a quick peripheral glance to see that she was furious.

'I am really sorry,' he persisted. 'Mum has suggested I let you take my car back to Adelaide.'

'Why can't you drive me home?'

'Did you see all the damage up on the farm?'

'I thought that was *her* place that was lost.'

Chris was losing patience. Sally had told him off for leading her on. Now he couldn't help but think he was an idiot for not telling her sooner. She was so self-absorbed and could control the universe with her sulking.

'Well, is that why you need to stay?' she pressed. 'To help *her*?'

'Even if it was, that isn't any of your business.'

'I can't believe you would cheat on me like that.'

'Sienna, there isn't and never was anything between us. I'm sorry I should have made that much clearer sooner.'

By the time he drove into town Chris was wondering if he might not have to take out a restraining order. She was beginning to look like *Glenn Close.*

'I want you to drive me back to Adelaide,' Sienna snapped at him when he got out of Joe's vehicle. 'You brought me up here, you can drive me back.'

'No, Sienna. My family needs me here. I have called the office and let them know I won't be in for at least a week. You may take my car back, and I will pick it up from you later.'

Strangely, the more Sienna pushed and tried to emotionally blackmail him, the easier it became for him to speak firmly and clearly.

***

The highly emotional "break-up" would have been enough to make Chris feel rotten for weeks, if it hadn't been for the loss and grief that needed to be faced by the local farmers. Tim had lost some outbuildings and a number of animals they hadn't been able to evacuate, but that was nothing to what the Nobles were facing. Sally had lost everything but a handful of stock. He'd only been able to watch her recovery from a distance. There was too much on their own property that needed doing, and once Sally's full family arrived, there wasn't space for him even if he'd had the time.

It had been over a month since the fire had burned through and though Chris had returned to work in the city, he'd kept a keen eye on the CFS website. The fire still burned in inaccessible country, and a recent flare up had caused the threat to escalate again, this time for towns and farms further south. Then yesterday, a band of monsoonal rain from the north had come crashing through the area and dumped three inches of rain. Chris had to acknowledge the irony as he saw the CFS website now listing call-outs to flood damage.

'So you sure about your decision?' Chris's boss asked the question as he walked in to see him packing his desk.

'I'm sure,' Chris replied.

'This about Sienna?'

Chris gave a wry smile. He thought of making the usual protestations, but it appeared that the office staff had bought Sienna's version of a highly imaginative story, and he was the villain in it. He was a "cheating bastard" apparently. It was his own fault. Communication—that was the issue here.

'This is about going back to where I belong,' Chris eventually said. 'I miss the land and I miss my family.'

'And things have been a bit tense around here the last few weeks,' his boss said. 'Wouldn't hurt to make an escape from it.'

Chris just nodded. Tense was an understatement. But the truth was, he'd only taken this job with the Department of Agriculture because he'd been running away from Sally. He'd come face to face with his stupidity and decided it was time to stop running. And yes, it would be great to get away from Sienna.

***

Sally sat in her camp chair outside her temporary home. Brenton's mother had loaned her their family caravan until all the insurance had been sorted out, and her home could be rebuilt. Her parents had wanted her to stay with them in their house in the town, but Sally

130

needed to be near her work. Her surviving animals needed feeding daily, and there was so much work to do by way of fencing. So they'd got a contractor to build a new shed with plumbing, connected electricity, and pulled the van up next to it. Home sweet home. It was going to have to do until they could rebuild. She was enjoying the warm evenings of late summer, just sitting reflecting on life. It had been a tough month. Every now and again her thoughts strayed to Chris Miller. Sometimes it was too hard to deal with, and at other times, like the present moment, she wished she could have got a hold of him and given him a good shake. Why couldn't he just say what he felt?

As if her thoughts had conjured him up, she looked up to see him walking along the drive from Tim's place. She wanted to smile, jump up and throw herself at him, bash him and scream at him, all at once. Too many conflicting emotions. She remained seated.

'Hey.' It was his usual casual greeting.

'Hey, yourself.' Sally couldn't help sounding just a little annoyed.

'Love what you've done to the place.'

Sally pursed her lips. He was avoiding the obvious already.

'Can we talk?' he asked.

'Do you think you could manage it?'

'There's no need to be sarcastic,' Chris defended. 'You know I'm not good at communication.'

Sally remained silent deciding to let him drive the conversation.

'I've quit my job in Adelaide.'

'Really? What are you going to do now?'

'Come back here.'

'Yeah, but what are you going to do. Can Tim's place support two of you?'

'It's actually half mine, you know. I just haven't been taking a wage from it these past years.'

'So it's going so well you can afford to come back?'

'Well, Tim has a family, so obviously his needs will come first. When it gets tight I intend to do some contract work.'

Sally raised her eyebrows.

'I have a neighbour who lost everything in the fire. I thought I might speak with her and see if she needed any help.'

Sally smiled. 'What if she can't afford you?'

Chris shrugged and raised his eyebrows.

'For goodness sake, Chris. Spit it out. We can't keep hedging forever.'

'I don't know where it went wrong,' Chris said. 'You have been my best friend since we were kids, and even when we went through all those gawky teenage years.'

'Gawky?'

'Well, you know how it is. Everything changes, and the guys talk about the girls.'

'Do they?'

'You girls talked about us too, don't deny it.'

Sally didn't deny it.

'Well things changed somewhere, and then I didn't know what to do, so I ran.'

Sally held his gaze for a long while, then took a deep breath.

'Well, if you must know, some time ago I stopped seeing you as just a friend.'

'Go on.'

'I started wanting to hug you, and kiss you, and sleep with you.'

'Sleep with me?' Chris raised his eyebrows.

'Don't be a smart alec. You know what I mean.'

'I do. I kind of had the same feelings myself.'

Sally couldn't help the smile that betrayed her attempt to remain serious.

'The thing is,' Chris said, 'I came to the conclusion that if we started…sleeping together…everything would go awkward. You know having sex with your best friend. It didn't seem quite right.'

Sally nodded.

'So, I decided that perhaps it might be better if we had a little official acknowledgement of moving beyond the "friends" stage—you know, with family and friends, and a minister perhaps?'

Sally couldn't help but laugh. She got up from her chair and threw her arms around his neck, and kissed him. Not the chaste kiss on the cheek between friends either.

'That is the worst proposal I have ever heard,' she said breathlessly. She saw the desire in his eyes, and responded. Their lips met again, and Sally felt bolts of electricity course through her. This time, *her* hands were everywhere, caressing his back and shoulders and arms, getting to know the man who had been her soul mate forever. The passion between them brought such a physical response in her that she almost couldn't breathe. Eventually she drew back.

'It might not have been a great proposal,' Chris grinned at her, holding her close against him, 'but it got the desired response, didn't it?'

A Piece of Cake
By Meredith Resce © 2014

I'm tired. Being the rock of support for the best part of sixty years has been exhausting. Wiping noses and cleaning boots; dosing illnesses and educating attitudes. It has all been part and parcel of the role I've played. I sometimes wonder if there will ever be an end to worrying about the family and how they will turn out. My plan was to be basking in glory by this time—applauding all the efforts and successes of my grandchildren.I have to admit that I'd harboured a dream that after all those years of hard work and sacrifice, I could sit back and feel just a little bit proud of myself. I can't help it now if I give a little sniff of cynicism.

I've got a cake cooling straight from the oven ready for my grand-daughter. She'll be here in half an hour, coming to introduce her new partner to me. What a disappointment she turned out to be. I know I shouldn't say it. Heavens! I shouldn't even be thinking it, but I can't help it. I don't know what was wrong with her last boyfriend. He was a keeper if ever I met one. Just quietly, I'm glad her mother isn't here to remind me how much I objected to him when he first arrived. Sometimes they can be so annoying, throwing up at me something I said yesterday, that I don't mean today. Good heavens! Haven't they ever heard of the idea of revising one's opinion?

***

She hadn't given me any warning. I'd known *she* was coming of course, and wasn't too surprised when she'd just burst in through the door and asked what smelled so good. I'd switched the kettle back on for tea, and was just about to slice up the fresh date and walnut loaf when I'd seen him lurking in the doorway of the kitchen. He'd looked like he was one of those hoodlums who'd followed her into the house: tattoos on his arms, piercings in very awkward places, scraggly, dirty-looking dreadful locks and a scruffy collection of facial hair as if his manhood was trying to make a statement, but his body wasn't cooperating.

"Who are you?" On reflection I suppose I must have sounded rude. I'd meant to sound threatening, and had a grip on the rolling pin that sat on the kitchen sink, in preparation to defend my home.

"Nan! This is Deakin." Samara intervened before I'd had a chance to swing the rolling pin. *Deakin! What sort of name is that?* Of course, I hadn't been much sold on the name of Samara, and had told her mother that when she'd announced her birth.

I remember ordering the hoodlum at the door to sit down and began to set out another tea cup. Samara had prattled on for a while about her studies and what not, leaving the poor boy to sit awkwardly. I'd felt uncomfortable for him and decided to include him in the conversation.

"So what country do you come from?" I'd enunciated slowly and loudly.

"Australia." He'd followed his answer with a grin.

"No, I mean before you came to Australia?"

"Nan!" Samara had objected. "He's indigenous. He's more Australian than you are."

Heaven and earth! A thousand different emotions had risen up to connect with loose thoughts, and had just about made it to my tongue when I remembered the many lectures I had endured in recent years on the evils of colonialism and that White Australia business. I'd decided whatever social attitudes I had been brought up with were not really useful at this point and so I'd swallowed them with a mouthful of tea.I had wondered how his name was spelled, and was secretly amused at the irony that the boy might have been named after Alfred Deakin, the first Australian prime minister who had caused all the ruckus with White Australia in the first place. I decided not to mention it.

"Why aren't you eating any cake?" I'd made an attempt to divert away from the gaff.

"I'm getting ready for pre-season training," he'd answered.

"Deakin's hoping to be drafted for the AFL." Samara had looked proud. "He's a really great footballer."

I remember hoping he would remove his misplaced jewellery before he took to the field.

"Well this cake is homemade, has walnuts and dates in it. It's perfectly healthy."

"He's on a low sugar diet."

"Why? Are you diabetic?" It had seemed like an obvious question. Samara had objected of course. He didn't seem to be too fussed, but merely pointed out that he was monitoring his carbohydrates and sugars. I'd got up and shuffled over to the side-board and picked up my silver fruit bowl piled high with apricots, plums and peaches.

"Help yourself. I picked these this morning." Apparently natural sugar was allowable as he neatly polished off enough fruit to leave a tidy pile of pips on his plate. I couldn't help but think that would keep him moving on his morning trip to the outhouse.

"Speaking of fruit," which we hadn't been, but it came to mind seeing the pips, "your father has taken my ladder, and I have six trees with fruit high up that I need to bring down for preserving."

"Well call Dad and have him bring the ladder back." Samara had completely missed the point and continued buttering another slice of date and walnut loaf. Apparently she didn't have any carbohydrate and sugar restrictions.

"He took the ladder to prevent me from climbing on it. He seems to think I have an expiry date."

"How old are you, Nan?" Deakin asked. I'd nearly choked on my tea. It was highly improper to ask a woman's age and further for him to call me Nan. But my dear granddaughter hadn't introduced us properly, so I'd fought for calm and forgiven him, at least on the one count.

"Well, I'm eighty five, and hardly ready to be put out to pasture yet. However, your father," I'd glared at Samara at this point, "felt that one fall from the ladder gives him licence to call the game. I need to get that fruit in before the birds find a way to get under the nets."

"I haven't got time now," Samara had said, as if this was her cue to leave. "We've got plans for this evening and have to get home to get ready." Deakin stood with her, and I noticed he picked up his cup and plate and took them to the sink.

"What about tomorrow?" I'd asked.

"I've got work! Look, give Dad a call and ask him. He was the one who took your ladder."

Samara had her bag back over her shoulder, and had grabbed another slice of cake as she was about to leave.

"It was very nice to meet you," Deakin had said. "If you like, I have tomorrow free and can come and help get that fruit in for you."

I'd had to flick through my catalogue of appropriate responses, and I could tell that Samara was reviewing her attitude.

"You don't have to, Deak." Samara had decided to break the moment.

"I don't mind. I can bring the ladder from our shed, if you have enough buckets for all the fruit."

Well what could I say? The young indigenous hoodlum was going to come and help me bring in the harvest. I should have said 'thank you' ever so politely. But all I managed to say was: "I like to get an early start. Can you be here by six?"

"A.M.?" Samara had asked, incredulous. "Seriously, Nan!"

"Sure," Deakin overrode her. "I'm usually up at that time anyway."

Well, you know that old adage—you can't judge a book by its cover—it turns out to be true. I felt like a proper old grump, having treated him with such suspicion. He'd arrived at five to six, and I hadn't quite got the cake out of the oven.

"It's a new health recipe I found in a magazine," I'd told him. "No butter, no sugar and wholemeal flour. I think you should be right with this one."

Judging by the way he polished off the whole loaf over the course of the morning, I surmised that the cake passed muster. He wasn't shy about eating at all, and downed about four glasses of my *Paris Creek* milk; you know the brand where the cream actually rises to the top. I hadn't had the heart to tell him that milk was expensive for a pensioner like me. I'd invited him to stay for lunch, after which he volunteered to help me get started on the seven buckets full of fruit. We had a lovely afternoon of pitting and packing and stewing. He was a little alarmed at the amount of sugar I added to the jam pan, but I waved his scruples aside. I've eaten this homemade jam for eighty five years, and don't appear to be any the worse for it.

I liked Deakin a lot. He dropped around a number of times, at first to pick up some containers of stewed fruit – the ones I had done with no added sugar. He came back later to tell me it was great to add to his home made breakfast cereal. Then he popped in occasionally just for a chat and a glass of milk. I took to making health cake just in case he should drop by. Then Samara dropped the bombshell. She broke up with him. I was so angry with her I could have spit.

"What's the matter with you, girl?" I'd said straight out. "Don't you know a good thing when you see it?"

That was when her mother took up her cause and pointed out to me my hypocrisy, to which I gave a sniff of disgust. I'm too old to be mending my ways. But Deakin was different. He was a good, hard-working, friendly and kind young man. I'd even caught a bus to watch a couple of his football games, and I think they should take him in one of the AFL teams. But no amount of protest from my side was going to influence my young miss. She has her own mind, you know. I wouldn't have put it past her to have brought Deakin to me in the first place just to shock me, and just when I came to like him, she decides she wants something else. She's a contrary one; probably not unlike her grandmother, if truth be known.

Well it's ten minutes past the time she said she'd be here, and she's late. But that's nothing unusual. I've made her favourite chocolate caramel slice, though I don't know that all of my cake making does anything to influence her decisions. Somebody else might see it as subtle manipulation. I tell myself I make it because she likes it.

I hear the doorbell ring, and I am immediately panicked. Nobody rings the doorbell here, unless it's a stranger. Grumbling, I pull myself up from the kitchen chair, and force my aching joints to cooperate.

"Hi Nan!"

It's Deakin. I reach up and pull him into an enthusiastic hug. But then realise that this isn't quite right. Samara is with him and she is grinning.

"What's all this nonsense," I bluster. "Fancy dragging me all the way to the front door when you could have let yourselves in."

"I didn't think that was any way to introduce my new man to you," Samara says.

"And that's another thing." I switch the kettle on as I go past. "Why on earth did you break up with each other in the first place?"

The young scamp, Deakin, lifts the lid on my cake tin to see what's there.

"I wasn't expecting *you*," I say. "You'll have to eat the caramel slice like the rest of us. Well?" I persist. "Why did you break up?"

"I asked her to marry me, and she told me to get stuffed," Deakin says, grinning as he pours himself a glass of milk.

I turn a well-formed glare of disapproval in Samara's direction. She pops the rest of a piece of caramel slice in her mouth and shrugs her shoulders.

"And?" I prompt.

"And I was tired of your nagging, Nan, so I changed my mind and said yes!" I see her cheeky grin like she thinks she's just trumped me. I pretend not to notice. I can hardly sit. I am proud of her! What a good girl she is. Already I am running through recipes that I can bake that don't contain sugar.

"Well," I turn toward my soon-to-be grandson, "I hope you're going to shave that beard before the wedding."

Best Seller
By Meredith Resce © 2014

When Kevin opened the front door, after having gently shoved Turtle to one side with his foot and picked up Smudge to clear the way of cats, he did not expect his life to change. It was as simple as that—the turn of the door handle, and opening of the door. Actually, half opening of the door, as there were three rubbish bags piled behind it. But that was the moment of impact.

Peering through the narrow opening Kevin caught his breath. It was a woman. He was not good with women, especially young, attractive women, and this one was a stunner. For all his linguistic intelligence, in the presence of a female he suddenly became lost for words. Blood rose to his face and his open-collared shirt suddenly felt as if it was buttoned to the top and strangling him.

"Mr Reason?" The professionally-dressed female on the doorstep smiled reassuringly but it only served to further muddle Kevin's mind. "My name is Clarise Norton from the National Bank. I wonder if I might come in."

Now Kevin's mouth was dry, and he hardly noticed the two cats vying for his attention, nor the presence of his terrier whose playful teasing of Turtle was repaid with sharp claws lashing out and sinking into Kevin's calf.

"What are you here for?" Kevin asked abruptly. Bending slightly and rubbing the spot on his leg where Turtle's claws had made a mark, he inwardly berated himself. He should have smiled and welcomed her inside.

"We haven't received any instruction from you."

Kevin felt confused and sifted through his memories to try and recall where he had met this woman before. The Bank. Yes, she'd just said so. What instructions? But none of these thoughts gelled into any intelligent response.

"In the last month we have sent four urgent letters that needed your response. I'm afraid it's time to consider what's to be done with your investment."

"Who did you say you were?" Kevin had seen the monogram embroidered on her jacket pocket, and the scarf that sported the colours of his bank, but he couldn't remember having seen her before.

"Clarise Norton. I'm the branch manager of your bank."

Without a grey comb-over and thick-lens glasses she didn't fit his image of bank manager.

"Norm Skinner is my bank manager," he said. "Has been for decades."

"Yes, Norm was your manager. He retired last week."

"We don't usually have home visits from the bank."

"Mr Reason, if I may come inside I will explain the situation to you fully. It really is quite chilly out."

Kevin's social grace was awkward at the best of times but completely deserted him as she pressed forward into the hallway. Obviously she meant to come in and make herself at home so he allowed her to walk through the cluttered hallway towards the lounge room just off to the left. He had never noticed it before but there wasn't a chair in the room that was not hidden beneath either a load of unfolded washing, discarded sports bags or piles of books. It was too late to pretend that this was abnormal. Suddenly he was quite aware that his house was a tip and the carefully groomed Ms Norton looked quite out of place in it.

"Did you read the letters we sent you?" Clarise picked up the sports bag from one of the chairs and put it on the floor before sitting down.

"I don't usually read letters from the bank," Kevin admitted.

"What? Why not?"

"I usually just file them."

"After you've read them."

"I don't read them. I don't even open them. They're usually just statements."

Kevin continued to speak as he walked into the next room and returned shortly after carrying a medium sized cardboard box. He tipped the contents of the box onto the magazines on top of the coffee table. There was a huge pile of unopened envelopes, all addressed to him, all with the bank's logo printed in the top left corner.

"It might take me a while to find the letter you mean," Kevin said. He began to pick up an envelope and pry the seal open.

"Never mind. I can tell you what it said, and then we can talk through what you will need to do."

"I still don't quite understand why the bank has sent you out to make a home visit."

"It's not usual bank procedure but Norm was so worried about your situation he made me promise I would follow it up."

"I still don't understand."

"Norm has been your financial advisor for a number of years I understand."

"He's been the manager and advisor to our family for as long as I can remember. He has basically taken care of all Dad's estate since he died; helped me sort out investments and what not."

"Yes, he told me. The thing is Kevin—may I call you Kevin?" He nodded and she continued. "You have been drawing from the investments for nearly eight years now, and not making any deposits."

"I'm living off the interest, you know, while I finish my novel."

"Yes, Norm mentioned you were a writer. The trouble is you have been drawing much more from your account than you have been earning in interest. Haven't you been watching the principal dwindle?"

Kevin looked at the pile of envelopes on the coffee table and raised his eyebrows.

"Yes, well." Clarise couldn't fail to see that his financial management skills were something akin to his domestic abilities. "The thing is, Kevin, you are going to have to take a loan until your advance comes in, or are you only receiving royalties from your publishing company?"

Kevin didn't reply. He felt the blood rise in his face, but couldn't seem to pull his thoughts together. He hadn't seen this coming.

"I'll need to see your contract to prove that you will be able to pay the loan back."

"I don't have a contract." Kevin's statement fell between them like a lead balloon. It took a moment for Clarise to respond to what he'd said.

"It's not really wise to enter into a business agreement with a company without a contract," she lectured. "For the purposes of this loan you are going to have to talk to the publishers and negotiate the terms of payment."

"I um…you see…I haven't actually submitted my manuscript to a publisher yet."

Clarise's eyebrows nearly disappeared into her hairline.

"I'm not really happy with it yet," he said.

"Norm led me to believe that you have been a writer for years, like before your father died. How long is that?"

"Yeah, ten years, but…you know how it is. These creative projects take time."

"Time's up, Kevin. It's time to get a real job that pays money. Your investment will only last another month if you spend at your current rate, and then you will either have to sell your house or find another source of income."

***

It had been three days since Clarise had dropped the bombshell on his happy delusion of security and blown it to pieces. She had spoken in a very logical and practical way, even offering to review his manuscript to see if she thought it worth pursuing. Though he had felt insecure about it she had reassured him that she was a prolific reader, and had reviewed many books in her time. Besides, the way she made it sound, there was little choice in the matter. Now that he understood his desperate situation and now that Norm Skinner was no longer on hand to advise, Kevin could not wait to hear back from Clarise. So when she reappeared on his doorstep again he almost reached out and pulled her into the house. Almost—but not quite. First he hurriedly did a mental take of how he looked. He'd just come out of the shower and didn't have a shirt on for starters. He saw her take a good look at his sculpted torso, and was suddenly thankful that, for all of his disorganised ways, he kept his exercise routine up. He knew what readers wanted their hero to look like, and he felt that he wasn't too far off par. Thankfully he had replaced the bathroom towel with his clean denim jeans. His longish hair was wet and dishevelled. It was usually dishevelled, but at least this morning it was clean. After a few awkward moments of Clarise staring at him while he did his mental review, he finally spoke.

"Ah, would you like to come inside?"

"I hope I'm not disturbing you."

"No, that is, I just got out of the shower."

"Yes, I can see that."

Kevin swallowed the lump that had formed in his throat and turned into the hallway. He grabbed his tracksuit top that was draped haphazardly over the hall table, and shouldered his way into it. Clarise was awfully quiet. He had that sense that she was fully checking him out.

Once she was settled at his kitchen table he managed to find enough sense to offer her a cup of coffee, and thank her for coming. It was then he noticed she was dressed in a pair of jeans with a figure-enhancing top. It was not her uniform but that was not why he noticed. He would like to have run his head under a cold tap as he needed his wits about him, not to be so overcome with stupid teenage-like emotions he could hardly swallow. When she frowned at him and then looked down at her front as if to make sure she had all her buttons fastened he realised that his staring was highly inappropriate.

"What's the little pink ribbon for?" It was the first thing that came into his head.

Clarise touched the little piece of silky fabric that was pinned to her t-shirt, and Kevin noticed she seemed a little sombre.

"In support of breast cancer research," she said. "I lost my mother to breast cancer last year."

"I'm sorry." Kevin felt terribly out of his depth seeing the grief in her eyes, but he was at least thankful that his faux pas had been forgotten.

"How come you don't have your work uniform on?" It sounded lame and he felt stupid.

"It's Sunday, Kevin. I've come around as—well sort of like a friend."

A friend! Forget swallowing. Kevin wondered when he would be able to breathe again. *I'm thirty-two-years-old and worse than a school boy.*

"I'm sorry to be so forward," Clarise said. "It isn't really any of my business, but…I just felt you probably need a hand at the moment, and I think I can help you, if you would like."

Kevin poured himself a glass of water and downed it in one gulp. What he felt he needed at the moment was a paramedic—either that or a good hit around the head.

"I read your manuscript. It's brilliant, Kevin. You need to believe in yourself." She was apparently oblivious to Kevin's emotional state.

He didn't reply. He couldn't reply.

"Look," she went on, not at all put off by his stupor, "how many bedrooms do you have here?"

"Four." He sounded uncertain.

"You use one for an office?"

"No, four, plus the office."

"Great!" She seemed really pleased, and Kevin could not imagine why.

"What about you get in some lodgers?" She must have seen his blank look because she hurried on with a well thought out pitch. "You probably aren't ready at the moment, but I…well let me be frank."

Kevin couldn't imagine her being anything else other than frank.

"My landlords have asked if I would allow them to break my lease agreement and move out immediately. I know I could hold them off by law, but they've been so good to me, and my small flat is actually their granny flat. Their father recently passed, and the mother is not coping on her own. They haven't got room for her in their house, and they really need my place, so…"

She waited and Kevin took a few moments to process all the information before he spoke.

"You want to move in here?"

"Only for a few weeks until I can find somewhere suitable. In the meantime, I am prepared to help you get all the rooms ready if you think you can manage having other people around the place."

"So, like a trial?"

"Exactly! You can see if you can get your writing done during the day when all lodgers are out of the house, and their board will help boost your income."

Kevin took his time to process what he was hearing, and wondered momentarily if he would ever be able to concentrate again. This woman was a powerful force over his brain.

"OK."

"OK?" She grinned. "If you find I'm too much of a bother, then we'll have to think of something else, but I promise, I won't cause you any trouble, and I'll help you with your administration, and getting your novel submitted to a publisher, and anything else you might need."

***

Kevin had worked himself into a proper sweat pushing his lawnmower over the knee-high grass around the yard. He used to mow the lawns back in the days when his parents were still alive, and he knew that running the mower over shorter grass would have been much easier than this. He had very much wanted to call in a mowing service to do the job, but Clarise had shown him the budget. There was no money to pay someone to do what he could do for himself. Then he'd been very tempted to just leave the grass to grow a bit more, but Clarise had talked so enthusiastically about how good the garden would look once tidied up, that he had complied without opposition. He found it very difficult to oppose any idea that Clarise put forward. She was super organised, and had turned the interior of the house into something almost unrecognisable.

"It's really taking shape now," she said as she stepped out onto the back porch, a glass of iced water in her hand. "If we can get the garden beds weeded this afternoon, then I can't see any reason why we shouldn't place an ad for boarders tomorrow."

"The garden beds!" Kevin hadn't moved past that comment.

"There are some rose bushes amongst all those weeds, and with a good thorough prune, they will come into bloom very nicely in a month or so."

Kevin had objections running through his head. She obviously intended that he would pull the weeds and prune the roses. That hadn't been in his list of things to do at all.

"I'll help you." She could read his reluctance. "We need to make a really good impression if we're going to charge top dollar for your rooms."

"You're very bossy, you know that?"

Clarise grinned. It was the first time he'd voiced any resistance, but far from being cowered she seemed amused. "I'm an administrative genius, Kevin, and you can thank me later."

Kevin just shook his head. He was half in love with her, but still wasn't sure how he felt about her taking charge of his life. As he emptied the grass catcher on the enormous pile of grass cuttings at the back of the shed, he did an inventory. The house was clean, tidy, and was beginning to look like a welcoming home. The budget was tight, but it was doable. His book proposal had been submitted to three different publishers, and he'd heard back from one of them who wanted to read the entire manuscript. His evenings were no longer spent sitting alone amongst a heap of clutter eating microwave dinners. Clarise talked a lot, but she was interesting and funny, not to mention beautiful, and she had urged him towards cooking and eating properly. It was both cheaper and healthier. As he fitted the catcher to the back of the lawn-mower again, he looked at what he'd achieved in his battle with the overgrown grass. He gave a sigh of resignation. It looked heaps better, and he couldn't deny it.

"Chin up, Kev!" Clarise called over to him from her position kneeling over a weed infested garden bed. "This sunshine is going to be great for your vitamin D levels."

Vitamin D! While he hadn't felt healthier in years, vitamins were the last thing on his mind. What was he supposed to do when she wore tops that showed her every curve, and crept up showing off the smooth skin of her midriff. She was gorgeous to look at. He allowed a stray thought to cross his mind and wondered what she would be like in his arms.

"Let me know when you're done with the wheelbarrow."

Her calling snapped Kevin back to attention. *Today we are gardening,* he told himself sternly.

***

As Kevin's house was only two kilometres from the university, the response to their advertisement for boarders was quick. Clarise had helped him interview the applicants, and before long there were two extra boarders in residence. Clarise had negotiated a good price for the rooms, which included breakfast and dinner each day.

"I'm not a very good cook," Kevin complained. "How am I supposed to get dinner ready for them every day?"

"I can help."

"What about when you move out?"

For the first time in their strange relationship, Clarise was speechless and a small frown formed in her brow. "I haven't actually been looking for another place," she admitted.

Kevin didn't quite know how to respond to this. He didn't want her to go, but had always understood that she would—or at least that is what she had originally said.

"Do you want me to leave?"

Kevin could sense something deeper behind the question, but wasn't quite ready to identify it. "I don't think I could manage if you moved out, if I am honest. You're an administrative genius."

Clarise grinned. "Ok then!"

***

Kevin hardly recognised himself. His two sisters had driven from interstate to see him and couldn't stop commenting on how tidy the house was, and how good Kevin looked.

"I'm so proud of you," his sister Alice said. "I don't know why it took you so long to get that book published."

"We really thought you'd gone to pieces after Dad died," Eva said. "I don't know how many times we talked about running an intervention on you."

Kevin was happy to let them talk. He wasn't quite ready to admit that someone had run an intervention on him. There was no way he would be in his current position if she hadn't.

"So this personal assistant who boards with you..." Alice changed the subject and Kevin began to feel uncomfortable. "Does he pull his weight around the place, or is he strictly professional?"

Kevin cursed the way the blood rushed to his face. Even though his sisters thought his PA was a male, he still couldn't hide the way he felt.

"What's the matter with you?" Eagle-eye Eva asked. "You've gone all red."

"Is your PA a she, not a he?" Alice asked.

"Yes, it's a she, and she has been the one who has straightened me out. She submitted the manuscript for me, she negotiated the contract, she sorted out the finances..."

"And she cleaned up the house," Eva finished for him. "Are you going to marry her?"

Kevin's face burned.

"Have you even told her you're madly in love with her?"

Damn! Why do my sisters have to be so perceptive?

"Kevin, you are so clueless. You have a woman who loves you enough to sort you out, and I bet she is still sleeping in the spare room."

"He's not denying it," Alice pointed out.

Kevin couldn't deny it. He had never been able to hold his own with his two sisters. How on earth was he supposed to work out the complexities of what existed between himself and Clarise?

"Don't be so backward, Kevin," Eva lectured. "This woman looks like she might be a keeper and I don't suppose she's going to stay around long if you keep calling her 'my personal assistant.'"

***

Clarise had been living and working with Kevin for nearly a year now, and their relationship worked really well—professionally. When she took charge of his bookwork and other administrative jobs he knew she would make it work and to his best interest. She did a lot of the housework too, but he had also lifted his domestic game. Just having her around was enough for him to realise he had been incredibly disorganised in the way he had lived previously; even to the point of being unhealthy. He wanted to show her how much he appreciated her input into his life.

"Wow, Kevin, this looks great." Clarise was referring to the table being set properly with a cloth and candle and two plates of well presented main course. "What's the occasion?"

"I just wanted to say thanks."

"How did your visit with your sisters go?"

"Good." His tone indicated that the *good* was half-hearted at best.

"What?" Clarise was nothing if she wasn't perceptive.

"They think I'm clueless, like I'm not in touch with the real world."

"In what way?"

Kevin was reluctant to say. His sisters were right of course. He was clueless when it came to the really important things. "It doesn't matter," he said.

Clarise got up from the table and gestured for him to stand up. He followed her lead, and when she reached toward him, he allowed her to take his hands and place them at her waist. She waited a moment or two and then pressed closer to him, placing one hand on his chest and fiddling with the collar of his shirt with the other hand.

Kevin's heart nearly hammered right out of his chest. "Is this just another life-lesson because you believe I can't read what you mean...or is this an invitation?"

"I've read your work, Kevin. I know you can read what I mean. I know I talk a lot, and you are very gracious going along with all my bossing you around..."

"Administrative genius."

She smiled. "I'm not going to make this decision, Kevin. This is an invitation, but you are your own man. You need to decide."

Kevin was not as intimidated as he had been when she'd first landed on his doorstep. He was used to her take-charge way of doing things, but she was right. He did know how to read what was going on. None of the characters in his books had ever been as reticent in relationships as he had been. It was time for him to take charge. He lifted his hand and cupped the side of her face.

"I've been in love with you from the first moment you stepped into this house."

"I know." She smiled at him.

"Well why didn't you say something?"

"I've been waiting for you to say something, Kevin. I can't control everything."

He was jarred from the moment as he considered how many times he'd wished he had the courage to make a move but had not. He was drawn back to Clarise as she put her own hand on his face.

"Well?"

He pulled her close against himself and covered her lips with his own. He didn't know how long, but for a delicious period of time he took charge of their relationship. The title, personal assistant, was no longer going to cover it.

About the Author

Meredith Resce, of South Australian origin, is currently residing in Melbourne. She has been writing since 1991, and has had books in the Australian market since 1997.

Following the Australian success of her "Heart of Green Valley" series, they were released in the UK.

Apart from writing, Meredith also takes the opportunity to speak to groups on issues relevant to relationships and emotional and spiritual growth.

Meredith has also been co-writer and co-producer in the 2007 feature film production, "Twin Rivers".

Meredith writes always with the hope that her work will encourage and inspire.

With her husband, Nick, Meredith has worked in Christian ministry since 1983.

Meredith is a bit of a mad footy fan (Aussie Rules) and follows the Adelaide Crows. In the summer, it's cricket – Aussie Aussie.

Meredith and Nick have three adult children, one daughter and two sons, a daughter-in-law and a grandson.

www.meredithresce.com
www.facebook.com/MeredithResceAuthor